BONE BLACK

# BONE BLACK

## CAROL ROSE GOLDENEAGLE

**NIGHTWOOD EDITIONS**

2019

Nightwood Editions
P.O. Box 1779
Gibsons, BC VON 1V0
Canada
www.nightwoodeditions.com

COVER DESIGN: Angela Yen
COPY-EDITING: Angie Ishak
TYPESETTING: Carleton Wilson

Nightwood Editions acknowledges the support of the Canada Council for the Arts, which last year invested $153 million to bring the arts to Canadians throughout the country.

*Nous remercions le Conseil des arts du Canada de son soutien. L'an dernier, le Conseil a investi 153 millions de dollars pour mettre de l'art dans la vie des Canadiennes et des Canadiens de tout le pays.*

We also gratefully acknowledge financial support from the Government of Canada and from the Province of British Columbia through the BC Arts Council and the Book Publishing Tax Credit.

This book has been produced on 100% post-consumer recycled, ancient-forest-free paper, processed chlorine-free and printed with vegetable-based dyes.

Printed and bound in Canada.

LIBRARY AND ARCHIVES CANADA CATALOGUING IN PUBLICATION

Title: Bone black / Carol Rose GoldenEagle.
Names: GoldenEagle, Carol Rose, 1963- author.
Identifiers: Canadiana (print) 20190088974 | Canadiana (ebook) 20190089083 |
ISBN 9780889713642 (softcover) | ISBN 9780889713659 (ebook)
Classification: LCC PS8607.A5567 B66 2019 | DDC C813/.6—dc23

To Terri Boldt

A wonderful auntie (even though she may not like to hear that,
which makes me laugh out loud). Such a dear friend and soul sister.
Love you so much—Namaste

**Bone black:** a term used to describe a glazing technique in pottery. Bones are burned at a high temperature to obtain bone ash. What is left, after being fired in the kiln, is calcium and phosphorous. It is white in colour. That ash is then mixed with iron or copper during the glazing process before the pottery is fired. The addition of minerals turns the glaze the colour of black. It is a unique finish, not often practised by artisans, and the process is ages old.

# BONES

Wren Strongeagle was almost killed by a train when she was little.

She hadn't turned five years old yet when she was standing on the railroad track. Wren and her twin sister Raven used to wander down to the tracks all the time. Some days, they'd be gone for hours after having wandered off the property where her grandma lived in the valley. They visited their grandmother often and eventually came to live with her. They call her by the Cree name, *Kohkum*.

The girls had a routine, especially in the summer. If they weren't riding their bikes up and down Kohkum's long and curving driveway, they'd be splashing around on the creek bed: a shallow waterway with a slow-moving current snaking its way between the grassy, hilly coulee of the landscape. Kohkum's house was built in the valley part of the land, beside Last Mountain Lake in Saskatchewan's Qu'Appelle Valley. It's an area protected by buttes and trees and an ever-present wind on the Saskatchewan prairie, but with a breathtaking view.

So often, as little girls will do, Wren and her sister got sidetracked and followed the creek in the direction the water ran, toward the big lake. A long lake. *Kinookimaw* in Cree. Back when Wren was just a girl, the rail line was still operational. Its tracks carried passengers and cargo from the city. The train wound its way along a scenic route of the Qu'Appelle Valley, right beside the water's edge.

Kohkum had always warned the girls not to play on the tracks alone. But as children sometimes do, they'd forget what she'd said and found themselves on the tracks anyway, picking up stones that they'd throw with all their might into the lake, playing a game they'd invented to see who could throw the farthest. It was usually Raven who'd win the toss, but neither of them kept score. It was just fun to be out and playing near the water's edge.

And the girls were never really alone. The lake itself was always busy with people enjoying a day of canoeing, fishing or just being out on the water. They were friends and neighbours of Kohkum, living in town a kilometre or so from where the little creek drained into the big lake. They knew the girls by their names, and would always shout friendly greetings when they spotted the twins playing on the shoreline. The girls would give a wave from the shoreline or the train tracks, and they'd remain there until returning to their grandmother's house when they started to get hungry.

On the day when Wren was almost hit by a train, a good day of throwing stones and laughing and waving at lake folk in their canoes, Raven had stopped to pick handfuls of sweet saskatoon berries along the trail that wound through the trees back to Kohkum's home in the coulee. But something sparkly on the train tracks caught Wren's eye that afternoon, so she lollygagged, sitting right on the tracks to see where that shininess was coming from.

She didn't even notice that the train was coming. She didn't hear its whistle, which sounded incessantly once the conductor saw the small figure on the tracks. Wren was enthralled, doing her best to pick up each tiny rhinestone she'd spotted embedded in the dirt beside one of the rail ties, and putting the glass treasures in the small pockets of her denim cutoffs.

People on the lake had noticed. As the train's whistle sounded in an increasingly furious manner, two people in a canoe near the shoreline yelled and screamed as loudly as they could at Wren. Still, she didn't hear any of it. It was like she'd been caught up in some other world that was bereft of sound and moved in slow motion.

It was at this moment that Wren remembers a bright light appearing beside her. She didn't know what it was, only recalls being thrown from the track and the oncoming train. She remembers it feeling like an electric shock, the same type you would feel if you were to foolishly put a knife in a toaster for half a second, which she'd already done in her so-far-short life. It was that little shock that brought her back to real time.

Wren remembers the sound of that train speeding past her a moment later as she sat on the dirt, now breathless, mere metres away. She finally heard the train's whistle and engine. She gasps even today, knowing that she'd have been squished if it hadn't been for the sudden appearance of that bright light, and the force that pushed her off the track. She remembers feeling the light checking on her once again, to make sure she was safe, before it disappeared. Then the wind carried Raven's voice to her, and Wren ran into the bush toward the sound of her sister calling. Wren was saved. By light.

On that day there was some kind of shift between two worlds, and for a few moments in time one of them stood still. That day on the tracks Wren acquired a special gift of knowing, which is how she has since been able to tell the moods of people, or to know things about them without them sharing any information, without even saying a word.

# ARRIVAL

Wren still thinks about that moment she saw the bright light. She doesn't know if it's a real memory. Did it really happen that way or was it just something someone read to her once from a storybook? Maybe a scene from a movie she watched? Her questioning of her memory happens each time she sees a flash of light, which is pretty much a regular occurrence—especially on these days when magic has again come into her life.

Three decades have passed since that near accident, and she's done so much living since. Wren suspects she might be pregnant but doesn't know for sure. Her period is quite late, but that can sometimes be due to stress, she knows. An appointment with her doctor isn't scheduled until next week. Wren's never been one to believe in the accuracy of a store-bought pregnancy test, so she will be patient.

In the meantime, she also looks forward to more excitement. Her sister will be visiting tomorrow. Raven is coming home. That's why Wren is in a big grocery store in the city, picking up some items so the girls can cook and chat and carry on as they always do when they find themselves together. They cook, they eat, they laugh—and so much more goes on in between. Magic.

Wren is reminded of the light when she sees a young girl shoplifting at the store. The youth looks to be no older than twelve, wearing an oversized, grey bunny hug. Wren saw her put some beef jerky into the big front pocket of the sweater. Her first instinct is to tell someone, but she looks at the girl closely, intuiting something. She can tell this teen isn't stealing on a dare, or as a bad habit.

*She's doing it because she's hungry*, Wren assures herself. It's like she is able to read the girl's thoughts. Wren examines a soft light that seems to be following the girl: light blue and hovering over her as if to protect. At that, Wren's instinct is to remain silent and carry on with her own business. *That girl needs food*, she tells herself, *and I will not be the one to deny her something so basic*. Wren dismisses the concern and pushes her cart to another aisle.

As she walks by the frozen foods section of the grocery store, Wren wants nothing more than to pick up a large frozen turkey. *It'll have to wait for some other time when we have a family*, she muses, smiling and patting her belly. Someday soon, she'll let her husband in on the secret she has been keeping. She chooses the Butterball stuffed turkey breast.

She places the frozen half-bird in the cart among a few other items that she'd selected: a bagged salad, some baby potatoes, potato chips, chip dip, a can of Spam and readymade gravy packets. She'll stoke the outdoor food smoker in the morning once the bird is thawed. By the time Raven is expected to arrive, it'll be ready.

"That'll be $49.87," the cashier tells Wren, without making eye contact. The clerk checks her long, red fingernails while Wren reaches into her wallet for some twenty-dollar bills.

*Sheesh, I have hardly enough cash left for a nice bottle of wine with dinner*, Wren thinks while counting how many bills are still in her wallet. *No matter*, she assures herself. *It's not like I plan on drinking anyway*.

But Raven likes a nice bottle of Malbec, so that's what Wren will pick up before making her way out of the city. She misses her sister's smile, their thorough and frank discussions, and she can hardly wait for the two of them to get on their bikes once back at the farmhouse. They'll let the wind run through their long hair as they pedal along the bike path near the lake, just being outdoors, like they always did when they were girls.

Wren hands over the cash to the waiting cashier. Out in the parking lot, while settling her groceries in the hatch of her small Nissan Versa, Wren finds herself offering prayers of gratitude. The twins have done well for themselves even though the odds growing up were against them.

Raven practises family law with a firm in Calgary. She was recruited even before writing her bar exam. Wren has travelled in another direction, choosing instead to express her creative spirit, completing her bachelor's degree in Fine Arts from the University of Regina. Her dedication earned Wren a place on the dean's list. She now specializes in pottery, creating what look more like sculptures.

The unique designs have attracted many commissions, allowing Wren to make a living as an artist. It's a career so many in her youth assured her couldn't be possible. "Be reasonable," her high school volleyball coach would say, "and choose something more practical." He'd suggest that Wren follow her sister into law or become a teacher, social worker or administrative assistant. "It isn't easy for girls like you to make a difference. Besides," he'd add, "no one makes a living as an artist. You will starve." He was wrong.

Wren couldn't stop smiling. This time tomorrow, she'll be slowly stewing up some wild cranberries. She'd had them shipped, by air, from Robertson's Trading Post in La Ronge. Nothing like wild cranberries to excite the taste buds. And they only grow in the north. The first time she'd tasted them was a couple of years ago when she travelled up there to facilitate a pottery workshop. The flavour has stayed with her since. Along with the turkey and wild cranberries, Wren knows that her sister will prepare her world-famous potato salad. Sharing recipes and blending flavours—it's what they've always done, adding up to everything in the world being right, just because they are together.

"I wonder if I should tell her the news?" Wren mutters to herself as she comes to a stop at the red light at the corner of Albert Street and 9th Avenue North, on her way out of the City of Regina toward her home in the Qu'Appelle Valley.

Wren wants to tell her she might be pregnant because she knows Raven needs to be reminded that there is still good in this world. It's news that might help Raven balance out the stress that's been happening at her work. In recent phone conversations, Raven has told Wren that a daily deluge of sadness, heartbreak and loss of hope has been causing her to lose sleep. Raven has taken on a case representing a Blackfoot family that is desperate to persuade police to reopen a missing person's case. Their daughter, just sixteen, disappeared two years ago while walking home from the rink one night following hockey practice.

"But there has been misstep after misstep in every area," Raven explained. "Police not properly investigating. The Crown not presenting evidence. The family left behind feels like they are being victimized over and over again. No answers, just jargon. No one seems to care. Like it's normal. Like no one cares about our girls."

Raven says their case has led her to others. She's been meeting with other mothers who've also lost daughters. "It's unbearable to sit and listen as they sob uncontrollably, recounting stories of sexual exploitation they've only heard about in their area," Raven continued. "A whispering campaign. No one in a position to do anything about it checks on the details. One day another child just disappears... People in the community tell stories about human trafficking, how it's a practice that is alive and growing, but police tell them they don't have the proper resources to tackle the problem. It's so frustrating for everyone, so there's a group of us trying to figure out ways to get people in authority to open their eyes and see what's happening. Maybe even call for an inquiry."

Wren thinks of a specific case her sister told her about the last time they chatted on the telephone. Raven was in tears.

"I won't mention the name of the family, but this case involved such a young girl. Only ten years old. She was walking home from school like she did every day, and a car followed her. Eventually, a white-haired man stopped the car and approached the girl. He unzipped his pants to show her his erect penis. The girl ran home as fast as her little legs would carry her."

Raven pauses for a moment and Wren knows she's likely lighting up a cigarette before she can finish the story. "The girl got home and obviously told her mom what happened. The mom called the police, but no one came. The next day, the mom made her girl promise that she wouldn't walk alone, that she'd make her way to school in the morning with the neighbour kids who lived just down the street. The little girl promised, grabbed her lunch bag and pulled on her sweater. The mom didn't realize the neighbours had already made plans for an extended long weekend and took their kids with them to an out-of-town wedding. So the girl was left to walk to school by herself. It was the last time anyone ever saw her."

"Oh my God, Raven. I can't imagine the guilt her mom must feel."

"Guilt, absolutely. She's wrought with guilt for not walking her daughter herself. But they had a plan to keep the daughter safe. Sadly, details of that plan weren't fully thought out. Her neighbour had always offered to drive the girl. It was no inconvenience because she was headed for the same destination. It was a standing invitation, and every now and then the young girl would show up for a ride. There was never a need to make a phone call to confirm. That's where wires got crossed."

Raven continued, "The mom is a single parent who needs to work to support her family, like so many other families that struggle. She needed to take an overtime shift that morning. A promise of overtime meant being able to buy extra groceries. So, she sent her daughter to the neighbours."

"Tragic. What did the police do?"

"Not much. They asked a few questions around the neighbour-hood. Didn't even issue an Amber alert, they just put up some posters."

So much stress. But now the sisters will see other again instead of just hearing each other's voices over the phone—and for the first time since Wren moved back into the old family home with Lord, her new husband. The old farmhouse is where the girls spent so much of their childhood, and is filled with good memories for Wren that she hopes her sister will feel, too. As she drives toward the valley, Wren knows this visit is exactly what Raven needs. It's what Wren needs as well.

# WREN

As Wren makes her way down Highway 11, her memory slips back to a mostly happy childhood, with a sense of joy in how she and her sister were raised. An industrial accident had taken Wren's father when the girls had just started elementary school. Their mother Edna used to tell them it was a sign that they were born on the date of a solar eclipse: March 7, 1970. The eclipse, a phenomenon representing darkness and light. "A day when elves play with ogres," she'd tell the girls. "There is peace in the entire universe."

Wren's mother had a colourful explanation for just about everything. Like the story she told and retold about how the girls' kohkum killed a bear using only a river rock. "Kohkum was out picking berries," the story always began. "She wasn't wearing her glasses and didn't realize that a small black bear had wandered into the same patch she was in until they came face to face. The bear snarled at her, but Kohkum had an arm like Ronnie Lancaster."

Wren can still hear the joyful sound of her mother's laughter every time she got to this part of the story. Lancaster is a football player who led the Saskatchewan Roughriders to their first Grey Cup win in 1966. Edna remembers that Grey Cup clearly, as it was the same day as her first official date with her soon-to-be husband, the girls' father. As the years passed, Edna learned to love the precision of the game of football. She said it taught lessons on perseverance and a belief that all things are possible. Edna would continue her bedtime story, in the exact same wording each and every telling.

"That's when Kohkum picked up a rock." Edna always smiled at this point while continuing to describe. "And threw it with precision at Muskwa's third eye." *Muskwa* is the Cree word for bear.

Edna used her stories to teach the young girls the basics of the Cree language.

"That third eye," she'd continue, "is like a baby's soft spot. And that bear falls hard. Coyotes watch from the bush. They are always watching, and they spread the word quickly: 'Don't mess with Kohkum. She's got a gift.' After that day, Kohkum was never stalked again while out picking berries." It was a story about believing in yourself— believing in magic and the spirit that surrounds.

Edna would tell the twins that she named them after birds because they were always meant to fly. Wren is the bird of vibrancy, alertness, efficiency; a pledge to make each day have meaning. Raven is steadfast and symbolic of change and transformation. Edna also started teaching the girls how to do beadwork before their sixth birthday. That's when she began learning, too.

"Other than creating beautiful designs," Edna would tell her girls, "it teaches patience and calls for attention to detail. Things that'll help you along the way as you grow."

This is how Wren embraced her love for expression through the arts. An early start. Now Wren creates designs with materials supplied by Mother Earth. Clay and pottery. Each time she throws some clay, it is a lesson in gratitude, because Edna passed only a couple of years later when the twins had just started grade three. The cause of death was cited as a heart attack, but Wren always figured her mother died from a broken heart. She remembers hearing her mom cry herself to sleep in the next room.

It's the reason the twins were raised by their grandmother.

"Rest in peace, Nikawiy. I love you—kisakihitin," she repeats in the Cree language, wiping away a tear lingering in the corner of her eye. Her musings have travelled with her all the way home. Wren unloads the groceries, loving the sound her heels make on the cobblestone pathway leading to the front door of the farmhouse. To Wren, it's a magical pathway built by *Mooshum*, her grandfather.

She and Raven collected the pathway stones themselves when they were girls. Their grandfather sent them down by the creek, instructing them to gather as many stones shaped like pancakes as they could find. It took days for them to find enough. They walked along the creek bed all the way to the rail line, and then back in the other direction right up to the outskirts of town. Good exercise, for sure. Wren can't remember a time in her life that she had more restful sleeps than when she, her sister and Mooshum worked on this project.

Once there was a substantial pile, Mooshum started digging ruts into the soil, little indentations big enough for each rock to poke its face up, just above the crust of the earth. He arranged the rocks strategically while the girls planted lollipops along the loose soil at the outer edges of the pathway. Mooshum joked that big lollipop trees would grow there in the future. Giant trees covered with lollies did not grow, but warm memories most surely did.

❋ ❋ ❋

Now in her kitchen, it was time for Wren to start creating more memories. She went to the pantry to retrieve flour, lard and baking soda. *Raven will love this pie I am making for her with the berries I picked last week*, Wren thought. After she placed the top crust on the pie, she carved a smiley face into the dough the same way their mom always did when the girls were little.

"Someday soon you will be a kohkum too, Nikawiy," Wren said and raised the palms of her flour-covered hands to the sky. She was speaking with her mother, now in the spirit world. "And I will tell stories about you. Lots of them, but I will change that bear story a bit, and tell this child that *you* killed a bear using only a river rock. Kisakihitin. I love you, Mama."

# SHADOWS PAST

Lord Magras is Wren's new husband. Hell of a heavy burden to carry a name like that: Lord. It was often the source of scorn for Lord when he was a boy, and especially as he grew into adolescence. Lord always wondered why his parents would give him such a name. "You are above others," his mother would tell him when he was young. "You won't settle into the lower class. You are Lord, meaning superiority."

When his class studied *Lord of the Flies* for a literature class in grade seven, Lord found his top-flip desk filled with dead flies one day. He left school and ran home crying to his mother. It upset him so much that she allowed him to stay home for two days. Lord was coddled to the point of suffocation. "I will always be here for you," Lord's mother would tell him. "No one can take care of you as I do."

People he met would joke about the name for years later. The only person who didn't was Wren. She didn't care about his first name and instead commented on his last name, Magras. "Sounds like muskwa," Wren said, glancing into his eyes for a moment before becoming shy and looking away.

"What does that mean? Muskwa?" Lord asked.

"Kohkum told me it means *bear*. A symbol of strength," Wren replied, this time meeting his glance and offering a smile.

"I'm not familiar with that term. And what does *kohkum* mean?" Lord inquired.

"That's the Cree word for grandmother. It's nice to meet you. You a collector?" asked Wren, changing the topic. "I'm the artist for tonight's exhibit. Thanks for coming."

Wren's new works were being exhibited at the Dunlop Art Gallery, located within the walls of Regina's central public library. A committed library patron, Lord had stopped in to renew some materials he'd borrowed but hadn't gotten around to finishing yet. As he strolled by the Dunlop Gallery, he was captivated by the beauty of the works in clay that he saw on display from the library's main atrium.

Once inside, he was taken with the beauty of the artist herself. He couldn't take his eyes off her full lips as she spoke about a piece she'd created. *Portrait of a Woman*, she called it. A large piece, abstract and twenty inches high, it swirled into many shapes capturing the feminine. A woman called by the wind. Lord purchased the piece that evening. Lord remembers her tossing her long black hair to one side as she nervously flattened a crease on her taffeta dress. And he remembers her talking about bears.

What happened after that first meeting was pure magic. The signs were everywhere. The day after meeting her, Lord came across a historical story about the lost grizzly bears of Saskatchewan in an ecology magazine. Then the movie *The Life and Times of Grizzly Adams* randomly appeared on a local television channel, and next a friend at work introduced him to something called a "grizzly" cocktail after a long week at work: bourbon, lemonade and an energy drink.

Only three days after they'd met, and there had been so many bear signs. Lord decided it was time to act. Even though it was after 9 p.m., and after more than a few grizzly cocktails, he dialled the phone with shaking hands, using the number from the business card that he'd picked up at the art exhibit. "As Lord of this manor," he said into the receiver, "I invite you to dinner tomorrow." After a pause he added, "Been thinking about you since we met." He said all this without slurring.

Wren phoned back the next day and ended up talking to Lord about what her style of art represented to him. "Perseverance," he proclaimed, "and always believing and never fitting into a box. Very bold. I love your lines." *He understands*, she thought, and surprised herself by agreeing to the dinner invitation.

Less than twenty-four hours later, Wren found herself checking out her reflection in the rear-view mirror of her vehicle and hoping that she hadn't sprayed on too much perfume. She insisted that they meet at the popular Cathedral Village restaurant in Regina rather than having him pick her up at her home, just in case her first impression of him was inaccurate. By the time she entered, Wren noticed that Lord was already there, sitting near the end of the dining area with a clear view of the front door. He was holding flowers—not roses, but a brightly coloured bouquet, the kind anyone can buy at a local grocery store. Lord did not take his eyes off her as Wren walked toward him. "You look lovely tonight," he said.

Wren had spent the entire afternoon primping and selecting an outfit, applying and reapplying makeup, and trying to figure out which accessories to wear. In the end, she was both stunning and elegant, wearing a simple black dress, long-sleeved but with an exaggerated neckline that subtly covered her cleavage, leaving room for the imagination. She wore simple jewellery, silver rhinestone-studded earrings and a choker-length silver chain that displayed a heart-shaped pendant. She decided not to wear lipstick that night, instead just dabbing on a clear gloss that outlined the shape of her lips. "Thank you," she tittered. "So good to see you again."

"I hope you don't mind or think it is too forward, but I bought you some flowers," Lord said, handing over the bouquet.

"Not too forward at all. Thank you." Wren sniffed their sweet fragrance before adding, "I can't remember the last time anyone gave me flowers. Oh, I mean, unless you count my sister who sends an arrangement each year on our birthday."

Puzzled, Lord asked, "What you mean *our* birthday?"

Wren's explanation led to much more conversation around getting to know more about each other. They talked about family, art, design and music before the waitress came to take their order.

"I will have your twelve-ounce filet mignon, medium-well, and a baked potato. Just butter as a garnish please, no side of vegetables," said Lord. Wren ordered a medley of sides that included hummus, tzatziki, goat cheese and figs. Lord found it funny these were all things he'd never even tried. After the meal, Lord insisted on walking Wren back to her car in the parking lot at the back of the building and just off an alleyway. "Just want to make sure you're safe," he said as he led her to her car. Lord held Wren's small hand and the two made plans to see each other again in a week's time.

"I can't wait for a week," Lord complained over the phone at about eight o'clock the next morning. "I'm sitting here, alone in my apartment and drinking a nice, hot coffee and thinking wouldn't it be so much nicer to be sitting here with you."

"Me too," said Wren. Lord suggested the two meet up again for dinner that night, but this time at Lord's home, and Wren agreed. Lord lived in a comfortable highrise apartment at the corner of College Avenue and Broad Street in Regina. Lord explained with great affection that one point in history it was where the edge of the city began. His apartment had a great view looking to the west, including an impressive sunset each evening and nearby Wascana Park.

Earlier that day, he'd stopped at a deli on the way home to pick up a ready-made barbeque chicken, some fresh ciabatta bread, smoked gouda and soft brie cheeses, and a side of quinoa salad—foods he'd never imagined bringing home prior to seeing what Wren ordered the night before.

They embraced that night and shared their first kiss. Lord recognized something in Wren as he touched her hair. Holding her face in both his hands, his lips were drawn toward hers. She returned the gentle touch and put her arms around his shoulders, a warm intertwining that offered a promise of something sacred and timeless. Their next kiss held purpose and went deeper: an unspoken pledge that they'd take care of each other's hearts with commitment that can carry and protect for eternity.

That's the story of how they met, and how they ended up living at the historic farmhouse today. They married at city hall less than three months after their first meeting at Wren's art show. Raven will be their first overnight visitor since becoming a married couple. There is magic when the twins are together, just as there is magic between Wren and her groom.

The farmhouse and its property had been bequeathed to both girls years ago—that sad day when Kohkum passed at the same time her granddaughters had been accepted to university. She wanted to ensure that love and tradition of the farmhouse would carry on, connection and pride of past and present, long after she'd gone to the spirit world. Kohkum's wish.

The farmhouse sat empty for some time while the girls made their ways in the world. But the magic returned when the newlyweds decided to make it their home. It was like the very land smiled and applauded. The hollyhocks grew taller and the perennial purple irises grew in abundance, thick like ground cover. The creeping ivy extended all the way past the trellis and toward the second-floor master bedroom window.

✳ ✳ ✳

Wren is so excited that Raven is visiting. Good medicine. She looks forward to the dim light of the fireflies as the twins watch from the veranda—fairies dancing, they would say when they were little. They'll listen to the lowly sound of trains in the distance and coyotes singing, crickets chirping and frogs calling out in what Wren remembers as a sweet melody. They will eat bannock, and honey made from bees that had pollinated the several varieties of wildflowers the girls used to pick. They'd give a bouquet of those wildflowers to their kohkum, so many years ago. In leaving the property to her granddaughters, Kohkum's wish was for love, a love that will fold its safety around new beginnings.

# RECONCILING THE PAST

Lord carries a curse. Or at least he's been told he carries a curse. He cannot bring himself to tell Wren that he feels an unease with Raven coming to stay the weekend in their home, their sacred space. He thinks, *It's amazing I invited Wren for dinner at my home at all. That I invited someone in.* Lord keeps remembering voices from the past. His mother's voice, and how she raised him to be afraid of anyone visiting. "They carry germs," she'd tell him. "You never know where their hands have been. Best not to take a chance."

Lord was never allowed to have friends come to his home for sleepovers or visits when he was a kid, nor was he allowed to play with classmates after school. A lonely upbringing. No colour, no magic, no memories like Wren's. No one but family was allowed to cross the threshold of the front door. Lord can still hear his mother's decree: "Strangers carry sickness. It's what killed your granddad. It's what killed your father." Lord has no memory of living life without fear of the unknown. It has become so thoroughly ingrained, it's more like a bad habit than anything logical.

But now he has Wren. And soon, her sister will arrive. Lord decides the time has come to tear down these old and imaginary walls and start building something that is real. He decides it's time to stop living two lives: one where he pretends everything is alright, and the other where his heart silently screams in pain.

Lord's familial roots come from old England. His grandparents were first generation Canadians. They brought with them hope and Victorian virtues, ways of doing things that were adopted, ingested and followed as rules to live by. The Magras clan moved to Canada in the late 1800s, settling in the Maritime provinces, an area where many families came from England, Scotland, Wales and Ireland. They settled in eastern Canada and called the powerful Atlantic shoreline their new home, bringing with them fresh dreams and old ideas, architecture being one of them.

There were no grand castles in this new land like there were in the British Isles, so new residents started building grand homes from stone. The statues of promise they built, old stone houses, could still be seen in Maritime provinces centuries later.

That is the kind of home in which Lord spent his childhood. It was a spacious two-storey dwelling complete with an oversized stone fireplace that caught the eye upon entering. That stone house, built by Lord's granddad, was tucked deep within the silence of a wood-lot in rural New Brunswick. Lord's fondest memory of his childhood was launching origami boats in a stream nearby the home.

How did he know origami? It was some after-school class in which his mom had enrolled him. Didn't matter to him that all the other students were girls. It's there he found his love for design. Lord constructed the paper boats with care. Later, at home, he kept up construction and practice. It was a solitary way of life for a young boy who was not allowed to play team sports. "This origami, it is a practice of precision," he remembers his mother telling him when he was a boy. "Good for learning discipline and paying attention to detail."

As a boy, Lord would spend hours measuring and folding heavy paper until it resembled what, in his mind, was a miniature tugboat. That's when his imagination would take over. He'd sail across the Atlantic back to his grandparents' homeland, landing at a port and unloading the multitude of fish he'd caught.

When he was young, Lord returned to England often, but only in his imagination. His made-up life included many relatives that he hadn't met at all. In reality he'd had a lonely childhood, as an only child with a single mom and no relatives his age. His mother's aversion to visitors only compounded his isolation. She would routinely remind Lord of the death curse that followed them: his grandfather had caught cholera from the neighbour who had helped build their house, and Lord's own father, a paramedic, had contracted HIV after attending to a bleeding woman in a car crash. The HIV worsened a condition he'd already been unknowingly living with, and a year later he officially died of bone cancer.

Lord's mother and father had hoped to raise a dozen children, but the family curse was like a creeping, dark plan from the universe, attaching itself to yet another generation. Because of his father's disease and death, the couple would have no other children except for Lord. Two generations had succumbed to illness brought in from the outside.

Lord clearly remembers the day his father died. He'd made his way upstairs and found his mother dressing his father's corpse. She'd dressed him in his Sunday best· a three-piece beige suit and his favourite striped tie. "What are you doing, Mother?" the boy asked as his mom propped up the dead body in a rust-coloured wingback next to the window.

"My love is gone," she sobbed, and she gently ran her fingers over the whiskered jaw of Lord's father. "We need to take a photo of this moment," she insisted, reaching for an old camera tucked away in a dresser drawer.

"A photo?" he asked. "Why?"

"Because that is what our family has always done," she said, explaining that taking photos of the dead began in Victorian England in the era when photography was first invented. "*Memento mori*. Remember, you must die," Lord's mother quoted. "Our family believes it will capture a part of the soul so that he's with us forever. A photo to remember those we love."

To Lord, it sounded like lunacy. The grieving woman asked her son to point the camera as she settled in beside the body of her husband. She had combed her hair and put on a frilly dress. She wore the pearl necklace Lord's father gave her on their wedding day. She set a kiss on the cheek of her husband as the young boy snapped a photo.

\* \* \*

Moving to Saskatchewan was an easy decision—nothing was holding him to the Maritimes. His mother had died the year before, and any other family that he was aware of lived abroad. After his mother's death, that big home became a lonely place for him. Lured to the prairies by a fat salary and an opportunity to start something new, he happily left. The architecture firm that hired him in Regina wanted new ideas with a twist of heritage, and his specialty was incorporating works of stone into new designs. His love of design led him to a new home, a new life and now, a new love.

# THE KILN

"It is almost ready, my love," Lord announces as he enters the farmhouse, just as Wren is getting ready to take her pie out of the oven. Lord has been working on a new project, creating an outdoor kiln for Wren when she works on her pottery during the summer months. The structure resembles a spacious igloo, with an electric kiln tucked inside.

Several months earlier, Lord had converted the garage into a pottery studio, including an area for display. He didn't like the idea of Wren driving to town to fire her work at the art centre, especially during the winter months when road conditions were often miserable. The renovation was a first anniversary gift. He had held Wren's hand and put a bandana over her eyes as he guided her to the new kiln. He'd made sure to install an oversized picture window in the studio with a view of the creek and the meadow protected by surrounding hills.

"Everything all set for Raven's visit?" Lord asks.

"Almost, though when you're done out there I wouldn't mind taking a walk. We need to find some proper sticks we can carve for a wiener roast. Raven and I have been roasting meat on a stick ever since I can remember." Wren has been smiling non-stop the past few days.

"Happy to," he replies.

Lord goes to the kitchen sink to wash his dirt-caked hands, a result of the physical work he's been doing outside. As always, he uses the nail brush to scrub the grime that's collected under his fingernails. Wren has always been struck by her husband's fervent hygiene habits. After wiping his hands dry on a tea towel, Lord hugs his wife and tells her he loves her. "Kisakihitin, you beautiful woman." He's learning words in Cree and uses them whenever the moment presents itself. He returns to discussion about Wren's new kiln, explaining the cement has almost dried—he's now just waiting for a delivery of wood.

Wren sees the new outdoor kiln as a herald of new beginnings, new traditions and new stories in the rich history of the farmhouse. She's always felt like the farmhouse was like a warm and comfortable quilt, rich in colour and memory. As she unpacks a new clump of clay, her mind wanders to places of the past.

The farmhouse is an old Eaton's catalogue design. It's been in the family since the 1920s, nestled in among a range of buttes and coulees that minimize the persistent Saskatchewan wind. The land is well-treed and a creek runs through the property. The creek empties into the big lake, which is close enough to walk to and enjoy a short, scenic hike. The lake is even closer if you ride a bike. On any given day, a family of deer wander by the property, usually gathering around the apple and pear trees Wren's grandfather planted years ago.

It's the perfect place to dream and raise a family, where Wren and Raven spent so much of their childhood. It's where their mother was raised. Wren remembers the stories she told them. Some of these memories are vague, because their mother left the family when the twins were so young. But so precious for the same reason.

"Your grandfather was a section worker for the rail line," Wren can still hear her mom's voice say. "The train used to run alongside the lake in the valley back then." Today, the rail line is a scenic bike path. "But because your granddad worked for CP, he was given a discount on shipping fees. Piece by piece, materials arrived on that train, and this home is what he built."

Wren remembers another story her mother told of how her grandparents met.

"She was just a young girl, out picking berries in Kinookimaw."

*Kinookimaw* is the Cree word for long lake. It's a place where so many love stories begin. An area where generations of First Nations peoples gathered and set up teepees. A combination of hills, valley and meadow. The landscape is stunning. Everything anyone might need grows in Kinookimaw: wild mushrooms and berries for harvest, roots and barks for medicines. No need for a drugstore here; the land provides.

When settlers came, they felt entitled to their newfound bounty and claimed the land that had sustained Kohkum's family. Abundant stock from the lake was overfished and their numbers dwindled. The animals that were hunted disappeared. Slowly, their way of life disappeared too, replaced by heavy steel ties that later became the rail line, changing the pace of what once was a quiet valley.

But those ties are how the family came to be—how Wren's kohkum met her granddad and how two cultures came together. Theirs was a legacy that began with creosote, sweat, hard work and saskatoon berries. As the story goes, Kohkum was completely focused on picking the plump fruit at the top of a bush. That's why she was startled when she heard a male voice ask, "What are you doing?" She hadn't heard the man's footsteps approaching and was immediately struck by the handsome features of his white face, blue eyes and welcoming smile. Kohkum replied that she was gathering saskatoon berries to prepare for a feast.

Wren squishes the hard clay through her fingers and once again hears her mother's voice in her mind. "Your granddad admired Kohkum's devotion to the land. He fell in love with the sparkle in her eyes. The same sparkle you have," Wren's mother would remark. "It didn't take long before the spot where they first met became their usual meeting place—the point where land meets water, across the shore from where the little arm of land meets the lake. That's where your granddad and your kohkum fell in love."

Interracial relationships were not common back then, and often not condoned. Maybe that's the reason Wren's granddad decided to build the family farmhouse just outside of town, though still close enough for a determined walk or a short car ride.

As Wren looks out at the land from her studio's picture window, she feels happiness and gratitude that her childhood memories here will be shared by another generation. She pats her belly and vows to go out and make a tobacco offering to the land. She will do her best to say it in Cree—Kohkum always told her that the trees want to be addressed in the old language.

Wren also vows that she won't tell Lord about the baby, not until the first trimester has passed. Babies go away sometimes, she knows this.

# RAVEN ARRIVES

Before loading up her bright pink carry-on luggage into the hatch of her car, Raven makes sure to include her pair of cowboy boots. They've been worn only once. She bought them when last year's Calgary Stampede was in full swing. While stylish, the boots pinch her feet, so she's giving them up. Wren can use them to decorate the fence post, along with that pair of granny boots Wren wore at their high school graduation.

Decorating the fence with footwear is a quirky tradition started by the girls' mooshum. Their granddad was the first to hang up a pair of old boots on the fence post the year he retired. He believed the gesture was symbolic of new beginnings. He believed that displaying his trusty old footwear, the very boots that helped him make a living and raise his family, displayed his gratitude for everyone to see. "The spirits will know," she remembers him saying. "It will make them happy and they will continue to bring good fortune." Sure, the boots got the neighbours talking, but before long, some of those neighbours hung up old boots as well, wanting to participate in something that added character to the landscape, and maybe delivered good fortune, too.

Raven looks forward to returning to that familiar land, to take off her shoes and let her toes sink into the soft mud of the creek bed just as she and her sister did as girls. Maybe they could even look for frogs, and at night sit on the veranda and listen to crickets. As Raven reaches for her cooled tea from the cup holder of her Chrysler, she realizes she needs this return to simpler times. Life in the big city just moves too quickly, even though studying law was her choice.

"Education is the new buffalo," their grandmother would say. Raven can hear her grandmother uttering the phrase as clearly as if she was sitting in the car with her. It's a saying her kohkum would often repeat, especially during high school when Raven toyed with the idea of dropping out. Her grandmother would remind her that before settlers arrived, everyone in the community had a role. Each held a purpose.

It's why she taught the girls how to harvest the land, why she passed on traditional ways of thinking: like women forming the backbone of community and family, and the a matriarchal rite of including the perspective of women in major decisions. Kohkum would talk about how white-man ways shifted this notion and caused imbalance. "That is why you need to learn," she'd remind Raven. "Don't let other people decide your path. We need to take care of each other, our children and our communities."

Raven decided pursuing a career in law would become her way of doing this, but it hasn't been easy. Lately, she's witnessed heartbreak and testimony about how families and communities are trying to cope with losing a daughter, granddaughter or other female relative. There are harsh stories about indifference. It still bothers her that an RCMP officer once commented that, "The problem with missing and murdered Indigenous women is drunk and angry Native men." Raven swears she would have clawed him in the face if he hadn't promptly left the premises in his police cruiser.

Raven is taking an active part in trying to change the status quo of indifference. She remembers the name of Helen Betty Osborne so often, and it breaks her heart. Helen was a Cree teenager who was found raped and murdered in northern Manitoba in the early seventies. Everyone in The Pas, Manitoba, knows the story. The community knew what happened but no one came forward for decades. Their silence condoned the murder and protected those who caused harm. Even sitting here, driving toward a much-needed visit with her sister, Raven feels uneasy remembering what happened to Helen. She sips back the last of her tea, frustrated that almost five decades later, not much has changed.

Raven is on a mission to help families and draft recommendations, suggesting ways to prompt authorities to reopen files, re-investigate and re-examine what changes need to be made to ensure the system protects Indigenous women. There have been too many stories about women going missing or being murdered, and a system that just seems to close the case file without seeing justice. More importantly, Raven is working towards something that will reawaken a collective consciousness. *Our women are sacred.* Those are Kohkum's words, and they've become Raven's purpose. It's why she looks forward to revisiting the land in the valley. She needs to spend some time in a good place and wash away negative energy with the healing waters of Last Mountain Lake. Raven was taught that natural water heals, even if it's just a puddle after a big rainfall.

Clusters of yarrow root come to mind. Kohkum used to pick them when the twins were teenagers. Kohkum would dry the root and grind it into powder to make a tea. With the careful instruction of her grandmother, Raven learned that the delicate wildflower holds the remedy to curing menstrual cramps, easing a woman's Moon Time, reconnecting with the gifts of Mother Earth. Raven guesses that work stress is causing her pain and a heavy flow this month. She could use some yarrow now and will suggest that the sisters take a walk on the land to look for some. She hopes Wren remembers how to gather and prepare the root because Kohkum didn't write any of this down on paper.

# IN THE SCRAPBOOKS OF MEMORY

Food. Home-cooked and prepared with love. Always a part of the scene when the Strongeagle women get together. Raven loves the smoked turkey that her sister prepares. It reminds her of the dry meat Kohkum used to make.

"I stopped using a barbeque ages ago," Wren explains while spooning some saskatoon berry pie onto a clay plate.

"Why don't you barbeque anymore? Seems odd. It's the closest thing to cooking over a fire, like our food when we were girls."

"Honestly, I am scared of propane. I had a dream one night about an explosion. Haven't used one since." Wren retrieves a bowl of sweetened cream from the fridge. The twins have always enjoyed their saskatoon berries this way, regardless of whether they were baked, served from frozen, or served fresh.

"You and your dreams," Raven giggles, taking the cloth napkin from her lap and attaching it like a bib, getting ready for dessert. "So, what's the difference with a smoker? It runs on propane, too, doesn't it?"

"Some do," Wren says, "but ours is electric. Just makes me feel so much safer. Besides, it's so easy. Turn it on, put in the meat and leave it. A few hours later, dinner is served." She places the bowl of whipped cream in front of her sister who immediately scoops on several large spoonfuls, her pie starting to look like a baked Alaska.

"So, what's up now, my lovely sis?" asks Raven.

"We put on our runners and hike up to the top of the hill so we can watch the sunset," Wren replies. "I've done it hundreds of times since you moved, but it's never the same without hearing your bad jokes."

"Sounds like a plan. I'll bring my Nikon."

"Last one is a rotten egg," Wren says, as the sisters lace up their runners and head out the door toward the prairie.

As they walk, Raven notices new invasive species of weeds lining the familiar pathway that snakes its way up the bluff to the top of a hill. She recognizes the common tansy, a brilliant yellow flower that looks pretty, but even cows avoid eating it, instinctually knowing it causes abortions during calving season. She notices an abundance of yellow star thistle, which is toxic to horses if eaten, and thick stands of purple loosestrife, which can overtake a natural habitat, choking out food and nesting areas for birds. *Kind of like people do*, Raven thinks. After sitting through talks with her clients this past week, Raven can't help but think that the most dangerous of any invasive species is likely people. She's still not relaxed from weeks of hearing tragic stories, but this visit is the exact medicine she needs.

"You know, Wren?" Raven begins. "The only thing that would make this moment even better would be if Kohkum was still with us. Bless her soul."

The sisters talk about their grandmother's guidance and how it has led them to where they are in life.

"She'd be proud for sure," Wren agrees, and then laughs out loud at a childhood memory. "Remember when we were little, and Kohkum first taught us how to use the stove?"

"I remember like it was yesterday," says Raven. "And even though we burned our first bannock, Kohkum ate it anyway, slathering it with jam and saying that the more we practise, the better we'll become as bannock bakers."

Giggling ensues as the girls remember wanting to be TV stars hosting their own cooking show with a focus on preparing picnic food from the tailgate of a truck. They would dress up in aprons and straw hats and pretend to talk into a camera, all the while preparing peanut butter and jam sandwiches with a side of homemade dill pickles. Their kohkum took a photo of them doing this one time. Wren makes a mental note to go through a box of old photos in her studio to see if she can find that picture.

The women reach their destination atop the hill, with a clear view of the lake and the land, just in time for sunset. During summer, the sunset is poetic, and the slow changing of light brings calm to both women. Raven announces there may be other changes coming in her life as well.

"I'm thinking that I might relocate back to Saskatchewan," she says.

"Oh my god, that is such great news!" Wren squeals with delight.

Wren has missed Raven's company and the quiet moments they've always shared, like watching the sunset together. Raven goes on to explain that the firm where she works has been talking about expansion. Setting up a new office in Regina is part of the plan.

"When will you know?" Wren asks, excited at the idea of having her sister close by again.

"Everything is just in the planning stages right now," Raven says, "and while I do like Calgary, honestly, it's just too big. Everything moves too fast. There's no room to just sit and feel at peace like we are doing now. Like we have always done together, right here on this spot."

Wren holds her sister, stroking her arm and marvelling at the sky-line that has turned from pink to purple to a breathtaking indigo.

"We need to capture this moment," Raven instructs. She sets her Nikon to the self-timer mode and adjusts the camera on a rock. Moments later, an image is collected in time. Two beautiful women, smiling and happy, the way they always are when they're together.

# THE STILL OF THE NIGHT

Wren is happy and content, especially tonight, knowing that Raven is sleeping just down the hallway. She feels further blessed waking up in the middle of the night and seeing Lord beside her. He is snoring again, as he always does after eating too big a meal. That smoked turkey brought back so many cherished memories, but through these thoughts of joy, Wren feels abject discomfort and pain in her abdomen. She figures it's because she ate too much earlier. There isn't even enough turkey leftover for sandwiches. Every bite of the smoked, oversized breast was gobbled up.

She feels a sharp pain in the lower area of her body and figures she might have gas. She gets up from where she's been sleeping and puts on the striped, black and white silk robe Lord brought back for her the last time he was on a business trip. As she ties a knot in the sash, she asks herself, *Why did I eat two whole jalapeño peppers the same way anyone might eat an apple? What's up with that?*

Wren had always made jokes about women who experience odd pregnancy cravings and earlier tonight, she was one of them. After dinner and two pieces of saskatoon berry pie, she had a craving for spice that wouldn't go away. Jalapeños were the only things she could find in the fridge so she ate them, even if it was midnight. As she heads to the bathroom, she thinks about the disturbing dream that shook her from sleep. She's had the dream many times recently. Now awake, she sees the vision again and it bothers her. It is macabre. She cradles her tummy one more time.

\* \* \*

Wren is walking through the meadow along the coulee outside her home. There's a pathway that follows the shallow creek and leads toward the shore. That meadow is quiet and fragrant, filled with wild baby's breath, wolf willow and the deep purple of delicate asters. *Purple*, she thinks, *is a colour that represents the calming stability of blue, along with the fierce energy of red.* Wren's kohkum used to tell her that purple is a colour that combines mystery and magic. But something is off. Wren spots a weathered scarecrow that looks to have horse hair covering its head in place of a cap. The hair flies in the wind. There's no reasonable explanation why a scarecrow would be placed there—there's no vegetable garden nearby, only a playground for squirrels and whatever other wildlife happens to wander along. As Wren moves closer, she notices the scarecrow is clad in a dress made of red and white gingham, like the tablecloth she and Lord often use for picnics.

※ ※ ※

She feels another discomfort. Chills and a cold sweat. She figures there's no point in waking her husband or her sister, but the pain in her lower body is getting worse. *If it's food poisoning,* she thinks, *why isn't anyone else awake now too, needing to head for the bathroom like me?*

The floorboards make familiar creaking sounds as Wren holds on to the handrail of the old wooden staircase. The sound makes her smile for a moment, reminding her of crickets and the songs they sing to each other at dusk. There's a night light in the upstairs hall, but this evening, its usefulness is replaced by a bright, full-moon beam of light that illuminates the old farmhouse, giving the impression of first light.

"Grandmother Moon," she whispers.

Wren can't help but wonder if her thoughts have caused problems to manifest. Thoughts are powerful, and obsessing about the negative can make the unthinkable happen. Her kohkum told her this years ago: "Be careful of your thoughts." It occurs to Wren that she's been preoccupied with worries of a healthy pregnancy. It's the reason she internalized signs of cramping, earlier tonight, while preparing the meal. She mentioned the slight pain in her lower abdomen to no one. Although she did feel a sense of dread and worry, she couldn't even bring herself to admit that fear to Raven.

Instead, she turns in for the night, still feeling pain and pressure. It causes her restlessness and sleeplessness. It is just before dawn when Wren feels a wetness between her legs. Spots of blood.

She silently makes her way to the bathroom, all the while praying her fears will be unfounded.

Her moment of calm is replaced with panic once she's in the bath-room. She notices an extreme bloat in her lower abdominal region where it hurts. She winces, trying her best to let out the gas that might be the problem but nothing happens. The only sound is the distant second-hand on the antique mantel clock, ticking its seconds ever so slowly. Wren decides to stop her efforts and moves to the oversized wicker chair that's been placed beside the original clawfoot tub. As she sits, she notices drops of blood trailing along the floor toward her chair. Desperate moments of agony follow as she realizes that the staining is also along the bottom of her dressing gown.

The pain increases, forcing Wren to hold the side of the bath-tub. She does her best not to let any sound come from her mouth, although what she really wants to do is scream as loud as she's able, to wake someone up. She's frightened. Blood begins to gush, stain-ing the entirety of her gown. She grabs a large bath towel and holds it tight between her legs. Wren moves to the floor and continues to breathe heavily. She begins to pray: "Creator, my heart, please spare this child who I promise will be accepted into a home filled with love. Please keep this child safe." Wren thinks her prayers might have been answered when she feels the intense pain stop. She removes the towel and a grief unlike any other weighs down on her.

There are thick, red stains on the towel and gelatinous blobs the colour of cranberry sauce. Wren stops breathing as she gazes at the towel. In the middle of the mess is a small figure, no bigger than the size of her thumb. Shaking uncontrollably, Wren removes the tiny shape, cupping it in both hands and holding it close to her heart. Again, she prays: "Please carry this child home and keep her safe until we meet again."

Wren sits there, alone, on the bathroom floor. She sobs. She finds it hard to breathe. She doesn't move until the morning sun shows its first rays, replacing the cold moonlight. Her unborn fetus is still cupped in one hand as she rises to retrieve a facecloth from the shelf. Placing the baby's remains inside, she gently folds the corners of the cloth over it. She doesn't want to shower, even though dried blood covers her legs. The sound of running water would likely wake up her husband and she can't face him now. Instead, Wren undresses, gathers the soiled bath towel and wraps the bloodied nightgown with it. Then she rifles through the clothes hamper looking for smaller towels and facecloths. She sponges herself clean using water from the sink and throws some on her face to wash away the stain of tears. She cleans the blood off the floor. She dresses in dirty clothing from the hamper.

As she descends the staircase, more tears make their way out. She's carrying the bloodied cloths with a plan to take them outside. She'll build a fire. While these items are burning, she'll go back upstairs and retrieve the facecloth that enshrouds the baby's remains. She'll put the bundle in her studio and make a little nest of dried wildflowers and sage until she figures out what to do next.

# DAWN OF DREAD

The early morning finds Wren alone and working in her studio, unable to return to bed.

*And what will these hills witness this morning?* Wren thinks as she, ever so slowly, wraps the tiny being in cloth, into a delicate, two-inch mound that reminds Wren of the tadpoles she used to capture from the slough when she was a girl. She uses a soft piece of red broadcloth to cover the baby she'll never meet, the baby she'll never see grow. Wren places these sacred remains in a small cereal bowl she recently fired in her kiln, the first of many baby pieces she'd planned to make. She remembers a story told by her kohkum years ago about how red is the one colour to which the spirit world is attracted. This morning, she hopes it's her kohkum cradling this never-born soul, her unborn baby, and offering comfort to them both.

Wren decides during these early morning hours that she will incinerate the baby's remains in the electric kiln in her studio. Her way of remembering. Maybe she will then make a colourful planter so that baby's remains will be a part of new growth, new life, some type of perennial plant like a lily or a tulip. Or maybe she will plant an aloe vera and use its soothing gel any time she has an inevitable kiln mishap that causes a minor burn. Her unborn baby could help her through that.

Wren reaches into a second swaddling of red cloth close at hand amid a wicker basket. Inside this new piece is a mixture of tobacco leaves and sage—two plant elements she uses during prayer. She asks for a safe journey home for the spirit of the baby who has left this world. She asks for forgiveness and understanding from the spirit world because what she plans to do with baby's remains is done from love. Wren decides she will add what is left after burning to the clay and shape it into a colourful vase. She will decorate it with an ornate design of summer wildflowers. The vase will sit beside the large window facing east, a place from which to greet the morning sun and new beginnings.

*But new beginnings for what?*

Wren brushes a salty tear from her cheek. Her grief is staggering as she throws a ball of clay on her potter's wheel. She adds slip casting and as the wheel turns, Wren lovingly fashions the middle of the ball with both thumbs so the round blob can begin to move upward into shape. Her tears flow fast now and begin to fall on her creation, becoming part of it. A memory in stone. A large-tiered and layered remembrance in clay for a baby she'll never meet.

Wren decides she will name this unborn baby *Amber*. To Wren, amber has the ability to capture moments in time, nature's way of preserving and calling witness to a single moment, a reminder of things that have come before. Wren begins etching that sacred name at the bottom of her moulded clay, still damp, when she is suddenly interrupted.

The heavy oak door to her studio opens and Wren sees the face of her sister. She is carrying a mug of hot coffee in one hand while balancing a plate of breakfast casserole in the other. Both the mug and plate are of Wren's creation. The casserole recipe has been in the family for a long time, something their mother made while the girls were young and something both remember as a Saturday morning treat while visiting their kohkum. The recipe is like French toast, but mixed with leftover bits from a smoked ham shank. "Never waste food," their grandmother would say. "It's a sin to waste food." This morning's variation is rounded off with asparagus, herbs and onions—all picked from Wren's garden. She notices the dish is sprinkled with extra cheese.

"Hey, you," Raven says. "Can't stop working. What's up, my lovely sister? What brings you to your studio so early in the morning?"

Raven's pretty smile quickly disappears when she notices the sadness that shrouds her sister's entire being. It's as dense as a wet blanket and just as heavy. Raven sets the food and coffee on a counter, then goes to hold Wren's face with both her hands. Wren closes her eyes, and another labyrinth of tears floods her cheeks. For the first time, Wren tells someone about being pregnant, but in the same breath that she isn't anymore. "Baby went away last night," she says, continuing to sob.

Raven honours the sadness of this moment, offering no empty sentiments, no *It's going to be okay*. She just holds Wren, letting her release the thoughts that haunt her.

"What if I'm damaged?" Wren asks, finding it difficult to speak through laboured breaths. "What if what happened before is the reason I couldn't carry this child?"

Raven hugs her sister even more tightly, offering comfort and knowing that Wren is revisiting guilt that she's carried from days long past—guilt about when she was raped as a teenager by someone she'd trusted, a secret Wren has never told anyone except her twin sister.

✳ ✳ ✳

When Wren and Raven were in grade nine, they often babysat for a family renting the acreage down the road. The dad was her school volleyball coach and the girls had no second thoughts about accepting rides home. But on one godforsaken night, the coach didn't drive Wren home. Instead, he drove toward the dump, stopping at the closed gates that had already been locked for the night. "I have some things I need to get rid of," Wren remembers him saying. He placed a worn set of goalie pads near the locked gate, as well as several black garbage bags that seemed heavy.

By the time he came back to the car, Wren saw the erection under his pants. She remembers the struggle, then the helplessness, and the pain. There were no witnesses except for a lone coyote on its nightly hunt. The coach drove Wren back to her kohkum's home like nothing happened.

As weeks passed, the coach no longer paid attention to Wren when she came to volleyball practice and she was never invited to babysit again. Just as well. In the months following, a growing shame and terror overtook her—she missed her period once, then twice. But who could she tell? Who would believe that a well-respected member of the community had assaulted her so severely?

Wren didn't sleep well those months. She stopped eating, only poking her food with a fork at mealtime and throwing the bagged lunches her kohkum made into the trash can. She isolated herself in her bedroom where she'd hug an oversized body pillow Kohkum had given to her as a birthday gift. She stopped combing her beautiful long hair, only bothering to pull it back into a ponytail for school. It was like living out a prison sentence, until she finally revealed the dark secret to her sister Raven.

In the days that followed, Wren took to self-mutilation, beating on her abdomen with hard fists and urging the fetus to leave, at the same time knowing that what she was doing was a violation of that gentle thing growing inside. Wren has no recollection of when the fetus left her body, no memory at all of the miscarriage. She'd blocked out that sad moment until today.

Not surprisingly, the coach was never called to task. Nothing was ever said, and the girls often wondered if he had made the rounds, hurting more girls than just Wren. He found a new job as that school year came to an end, and he and his family relocated to Ontario. Wren never saw him again.

※ ※ ※

"But I thought that all that ever happened to you was bruising when you hit yourself," says Raven, trying her best to console. "I've never thought you carried a child. You never talked about a miscarriage. There would have been some kind of trauma that you'd remember coming from your body." After a moment, she continues, "God does not punish the innocent, not in that case and not in this one. The innocent one is you, my dear sister." Raven wraps her arms around Wren even tighter.

"I need to tell Lord," Wren suddenly says.

"Maybe," counsels Raven, "but not right now. Give it some time. I want you to make peace with yourself before going to pieces again. And always remember, God does not punish the innocent." Then after a moment she asks, "Are you sure it's a good idea to transform those remains into something you are likely to look at every day?"

"I'm sure," Wren promises. "This sweet little angel will be remembered with dignity. Plus," she says, "I don't see it as any different from all the people who keep ashes of their loved ones in an urn on the mantel. She brought moments of joy to me and she will continue to bring joy, even if she's now in the spirit world."

# THE RED CRAVAT

Instead of drinking the coffee she'd brought, Raven suggests her sister have some chamomile tea, out of the studio and away from the sadness that she'd been sculpting in clay. "Let's go in the house," she suggests. In the warmth of the farmhouse kitchen, Raven puts on the kettle. "Here," Raven offers once tea is steeped. "To settle your stomach and help you get some rest." She hands Wren a steaming mug.

"What's this?" Raven picks up a note left on the large kitchen island. It says, *Didn't want to disturb you and Raven reminiscing in your studio, so I took some breakfast to go. Miss you already and see you in a few days, my love.*

This may be the first time Wren really wishes her husband was staying with her at home instead of travelling. He was off on an early flight to Calgary again, since he'd just secured a contract with his old firm to design stone guest houses at one of the mountain lodges in Alberta. He'd be gone until Wednesday.

"Well, *I'm* here with you," Raven says, "and I will extend my visit until Thursday, or even Friday, just to make sure I'm not leaving you alone. We'll have fun. Maybe jump in the lake later this afternoon. Check out some garage sales."

Wren agrees that it sounds like a good plan. She figures that healing waters may help heal her broken heart.

"But before we do anything," Raven says, "I'm going to suggest you head upstairs and try to lay down for a bit. I'll clean up the kitchen and figure out something to eat later for lunch. You need some sleep."

Raven casts a glance toward the stairwell, hoping Wren will honour her wishes. Wren agrees, sighs and gently holds the hand rail as she makes her way up to the bedroom.

As Raven begins washing dishes, she notices the local newspaper laying on the counter. She dries her hands and starts leafing through the pages. It makes her smile to read stories of the small community. Two young boys rescued a fawn, left abandoned after its mother was hit by a car. The boys wrapped her in a towel and brought her home. Their efforts made sure the little animal was sent to a wildlife sanctuary in Moose Jaw.

Raven reads another story about residents in the town gathering at the community hall to celebrate someone's ninetieth birthday, a beautiful old woman who carries knowledge and appreciation for the land. There is another a story about a dinner-theatre production being staged in the school gym, evidence that local community members embrace the arts. Amidst the headlines, Raven notices an ad:

At first glance, Raven scoffs. *Why would anyone admit being a redneck, let alone celebrate it?* She changes her thinking though, after only a few short moments, realizing that mindless gaiety in a social setting might be just what Wren might need. Especially since Lord is away.

Silliness will give Wren a chance to snicker at those who are bold enough to black out their front teeth and don a pair of tattered overalls rolled up to the knee. The party is tomorrow night. Raven makes a mental note to mention it to her sister after she's had a chance to rest. Besides, the ad also says there will be a special price on chicken wings and a live band. Who doesn't appreciate chicken wings and live music?

Wren is surprised she falls asleep so quickly once tucked into her comfortable bed, but with the sleep comes something else: her recurring dream. Wren tosses and turns, sweating as she once again finds herself walking toward the meadow and the mysterious scarecrow. This time the dummy moves, extending one hand and bending toward the ground. It captures a baby bird, just new from its nest and learning to fly.

The straw fingers turn hard and pliable like steel threads, encasing the small bird, which begins squawking with fear. Close by, the mother bird screams in protest but the scarecrow doesn't flinch, it just keeps on squeezing. Wren notices the attire on the figure is altered from her last dream in this pasture. Now it wears a red cravat tucked in amongst the gingham.

Wren awakes with a start, kicking off the light sheet that's covering her. She realizes she's seen that neck scarf before. It's in the photo of Lord's mother. That photo taken of her the day of her funeral, just as she had taken one of Lord's deceased father: a photo of the old woman lying dead in her coffin, part of a long-standing tradition in the Magras family to take photos of the dead.

# DISPLACEMENT

Wren and Lord rarely disagree on anything. It's the way it's been since the first day they met. If there is conflict, it's always smoothed over with some discussion and sensible logic. They talk about and share their feelings. They are honest and vulnerable; it's what holds them together—there's nothing phony or unspoken between them.

Wren remembers Lord telling her he hated asparagus the first time she cooked him a meal. He'd used his fork to push the vegetable to the side of his plate. "You might like to try it," she'd urged. "I grow it myself and toss it with garlic, butter, parmesan and black pepper. It's one of my favourites."

Most probably, Lord was trying to make a good impression because it was early in their relationship, so he did put a forkful in his mouth. Surprised, Wren was correct, the flavour was superb. Now asparagus is something he asks for as a side dish on a regular basis.

She's changed his view with respect to other, simple considerations as well. Like decorating the farmhouse. When the couple first moved in, Wren suggested they brighten up some of the rooms with a new paint job. Watching HGTV had turned Wren into a fan of the "accent wall," which is what she'd had in mind for the downstairs family room. Other than the kitchen, that room was likely to be a room where the newlyweds would spend a lot of their time. The huge bay window and window seat frames a view that looks toward the west, catching the evening sunset. An antique, cast iron wood stove was still in good working order and the main source of heat during the winter months. The room had a bookshelf built-in from floor to ceiling and spanning an entire wall. Wren wants to spruce it up with a new coat of paint, and she suggests a shade of orange.

"Oh, yikes," Lord responded when she told him her plan. "I've always regarded orange as such an offensive colour. I never use it in my designs."

"Kohkum always told me that orange represents energy." Wren shows Lord a swatch of a hue she's hoping to use. "Just an accent wall," she assures him. She explains that orange reminds her of the sunset, and how the colour captures the essence of her favourite season, autumn. She even mentions that, spiritually speaking, orange is the colour of a person's aura when they're radiating happiness, joy, vibrancy and warmth.

Her descriptions come from a place of memory and love, which softens Lord's heart. It's what he also wants for their home and he changes his attitude toward the colour. Now, that orange hue is what catches the soft lighting of the wood stove when the two cuddle up for an evening of relaxation and a good movie.

The dream prompts Wren with an uncomfortable idea, one that may require her to navigate through another potential disagreement. When Lord returns, she will ask him once again if she can move the display photo of his mom that sits on the mantel in the living room. That framed photo of Lord's mother laying in her coffin is something Wren has always had a hard time getting used to. Even the idea of death photography is unsettling for her, despite Lord telling her that it was the norm in certain parts of the Maritimes and the New England states, and even still happens today.

Lord has always honoured her Cree roots, so even though the image of a dead woman on her mantel gives her the willies, she feels a bit conflicted. She wants to be able to honour his family's traditions in return. She hasn't been able to tell him that the photo seems haunted.

And now the dream, the red cravat. At times, she's felt as if the eyes of Lord's dead mother are open and watching her from the photo, and she has yet to tell him about the disconcerting thing that happened one night when he was away.

✳ ✳ ✳

There was a wicked rainstorm in the valley and Lord was gone again for work. As Wren settled in for the night, lighting a fire in the stone fireplace, she felt as though she was being watched. Maybe it was the sound of a harsh wind blowing branches against the side of the house. Maybe it was the flickering of light from the fireplace. Maybe it was the fact that Wren was alone and in a large home out in the middle of the prairie. Maybe her eyes were playing tricks on her but in those moments, Wren was certain she saw the eyes in the death photo open. She shook her head in disbelief and looked again. The eyes were closed. But were they open a moment before?

※ ※ ※

Awake from her nightmare, Wren remembers noticing the cravat in the photo and thinking, *What an odd piece of clothing to take to one's final resting place.*

Lord had given no direct answer to an earlier request by Wren to move the photo, feeling as though he was being asked to make a choice between his love for Wren and love for his mother. He side-stepped the subject instead, offering to make them both tea and some microwave popcorn.

Wren has never told her husband about the eerie quality of the photo. How does she explain the darkness she's felt from it? It's even disturbing Kohkum's love in this home. Energy is real and Wren believes the presence of that photo causes disruption.

# THE DAY AFTER

The next morning, the sisters are wakened by the sounds of air brakes coming to a halt. Wren pulls back the bedroom curtains to see a couple of young farm boys in the yard. She knows them, giving a smile and wave before hurriedly pulling on a pair of sweatpants and a sweater of Lord's that she finds on the floor. It's two sizes too big for Wren and fits her more like a dress. "Comfort clothing" she calls it. Wren likes wearing her husband's clothing when he's away because the fabric holds his scent.

The neighbour boys are delivering the first cord of firewood that Lord ordered before leaving on his trip. Wren admires them both as they are always so polite and respectful. Their family owns the nursery up the highway, the place where she buys her seedlings. Within minutes, Wren is outside to say hello to them, and to see if they want any help with unloading.

"Morning, Miss. It's going to be a hot one today," the blond-haired lad offers as Wren steps out the front door. "Thought we'd get this chore out of the way before the morning breaks."

He and his brother offer to stack the wood.

"No need," replies Wren. "We can stack it if you just unload it. My sister is visiting," she adds, "so we can do it. Nice to have some company as my husband is away on business again."

"Sure is enough for a lot of bonfires," the boy remarks. "A lot of fire."

Working together, the boys seem to unload the entire cord within minutes, offering final goodbyes and waves as they swing back into their green pickup and retreat down the grid leading to the main highway.

All this activity happens before Raven has mustered up the gumption to get out of bed and join her sister outside. When she appears, she's carrying two mugs of hot coffee. "Good thing you set the timer on this last night," Raven says and yawns, handing over one of the coffees to her sister. "I can't imagine starting the day without it." It's then she notices the big pile of freshly chopped wood, which appears to be blocking her car in the driveway. "Where did this come from?" she asks.

Wren chuckles and motions to Raven to follow her to the side of the house. The mortar is now dried on Wren's new outdoor kiln.

"It's lovely," Raven says as she observes Lord's handiwork in building it, "but why do you need another one? You already have a kiln in your studio."

Wren explains, "When it's hot out and I'm wanting to fire my work, it's almost unbearable to be working inside." She describes how, one morning not long ago, Lord had come home to find Wren taking a cold shower just to cool down. Firing the kiln had made her studio as hot as an oven. "It was after that day he started with plans for this outdoor model. A gift, he said, for our first anniversary."

"You firing it up this weekend?" Raven asks.

"Hadn't planned on it ..." starts Wren.

"Good," Raven interjects, "because I have a plan. Tell you all about it in a few minutes. Let's head in for some breakfast first."

While the two walk back to the farmhouse, Wren finds herself feeling content and rested. A night has passed since the baby went away, but Wren has the comfort of her sister keeping her heart safe, even if her sleep has been interrupted by that recurring and macabre dream about the scarecrow and red cravat. She figures it's because the two have been joking about old times, and is there such a thing as too much fresh air?

The twins have walked in the meadow and along the banks of the stream, just like they did when they were girls, picking rocks and wildflowers. Wren finds the familiarity brings her calm. This morning, she notices Raven does not bring up the subject of the baby going away, which is just as well. It will take some time for Wren to accept what happened, and even more time to decide whether to let her husband know.

Later, while the two are stacking cordwood, Raven mentions the shindig happening down at the local watering hole. "Come on, we should go," Raven urges. "It'll do you some good. Besides, it will give me a chance to meet some of the characters in town who you've been describing."

It's hard to say no to some harmless activity aimed at cheering her up, so Wren agrees; before long, the two find themselves in the basement of the farmhouse digging through old clothes that might serve as redneck attire.

"I stored all my fat clothes down here," Wren admits. "You know the ones."

Raven nods. She does indeed know the practice of keeping over-sized clothing in the closet, just in case.

"I've been meaning to send these to the Sally Ann for a while now," Wren says about the clothes.

"Well, good thing you didn't. We can find some redneck costume items in here for that party, I'm sure. As Raven rifles through a black garbage bag of clothes, she snickers at some of the styles. Just then, Wren notices a piece of clothing that she knows she didn't put down there: a red and white gingham dress, the same style that she's seen on the scarecrow in her dreams.

*Where did it come from?*

# WILD WEST

The sisters are clad in oversized jeans, tied at the waist with a piece of rope, and tartan flannel shirts from their teenage days as Bay City Rollers fans. Redneck enough? Doesn't matter. There are chicken wings to be enjoyed.

As Wren pulls her car into the parking lot, the women let out a roar of laughter. "We've certainly come to the right place," Wren exclaims, having a hard time speaking while laughing at a crude display hanging from the back of another vehicle.

"I can't believe anyone would display something like that and actually go out in public!" cries Raven. A pair of silver bull balls dangle from the back the truck's bumper. There is nowhere else to park, so they park right next to it, a blue beat-up pickup. Wren makes a mental note to memorize the plate number, a game she plays with herself to keep her mind sharp.

The place is packed. They go in, find a table, and order a plate of "Rajin Cajun" hot wings but before they can place a drink order, a second server shows up and sets two oversized cocktails in front of them.

"Wow. First drink on the house?" Raven asks.

"No, it's compliments of the gentleman over in the corner," she replies. Both ladies try to see who the benefactor is, but the crowd obscures their view. "Tell him thanks, from us both," Wren says, and studies the intricate drink.

"Call me crazy, but I always thought that drinking from a fishbowl was more of a cosmopolitan thing than a redneck thing," Raven says before taking a sip of her oversized cocktail.

"It's actually more of a bachelorette-in-Vegas type thing," Wren replies and snickers.

Oversized fishbowl or not, the price—and flavour—was right: three shots of vodka served with cranberry juice, soda water and slices of fresh strawberries floating in ice and topped with a slice of orange peel. Two fishbowls later and the sisters put in another food order. Salt and pepper wings this time. They haven't had much opportunity to talk because of how loud it is in the bar.

"Know any of these people?" Raven is able to yell to her between terrible renditions by the *band* on stage.

"No... I'm going to run to the little girls' room. Do you want me to get anything as I make my way back?" Wren asks before grabbing her purse.

"Nothing, thanks. I'll just sit and watch," Raven shouts in response.

As Wren scurries away and Raven takes another sip, she's startled when a man whispers into her ear, "Nice bandana. Wanna see my banana?"

*What a comment to utter to a lady!* Her instinct is to turn and give this intruder a hard, verbal lashing, maybe even slap him across the face. Raven turns toward the voice to make her disapproval clear but changes her mind immediately. The fellow standing there is incredibly handsome.

"Sorry about that cheesy line, but it *is* redneck night." The man introduces himself as Lance. "Seriously though, you just won me twenty dollars. My friend over there bet me that you'd slap my face saying something like that. Thanks for making him the loser."

Raven laughs, admitting, "Well, you almost did get hit in the face, but there are too many witnesses here. Besides, we don't want to get thrown out of the bar."

"It's often more fun to party out here instead of in the city," Lance explains. "Especially during the summer. Everyone is so friendly." He tells Raven he delivers furniture for one of the larger stores in the city.

As Lance and Raven continue to chat, it isn't his words that grab Raven's attention, it's his low-cut wife beater. The white undershirt fits him just a bit too tight and shows off his muscular chest and arms. He reminds her of a young Richard Gere.

"Smoke?" Lance pulls a worn, silver cigarette case from his back pocket. "Keeps the smokes from getting squished. It used to belong to my dad. Took it with him when he'd go hunting." Lance glances at the worn lettering engraved across the front. "I know it's a bad habit, but now that the band has taken a break, seems like a good time to head outdoors," he adds. "I'll be back in just a few minutes, if it's okay to join you when I return."

"Actually, I think I'll come out, too. Hardly anyone smokes anymore and it's more interesting to have company than just lighting up and standing outside alone. Besides, my sister is in the washroom. I may as well grab the opportunity to sneak out before she has time to give me a lecture."

Raven's been craving a cigarette all evening. She's not allowed to smoke in the farmhouse and isn't comfortable standing outside by herself all the time, especially at night in the dark. In the city when she smokes at her own apartment, it's usually out on the balcony where she can see streetlights, people and automobiles at every hour.

Raven realizes how much she appreciates being back in the stillness of the valley. It's beautiful and brings her comfort. Being here takes her back to her childhood. She's happy about the prospect of relocating back to the land she knows and loves, should the law firm she works for expands into Saskatchewan as planned.

Raven grabs her purse from the back of her chair. She leaves her sweater because the night air is still warm. No one notices Raven walk out toward the exit with some handsome stranger she's just met. All attention has turned to an arm-wrestling competition that has just started up.

# EMPTY CHAIRS AND EMPTY TABLES

It's Saturday morning and Wren is frantic on the telephone with Lord. It hasn't been easy to reach him because cellphone connections are sometimes tenuous in the mountains, especially if the weather is bad. Plus there's been a thunderstorm. It started shortly after his plane landed yesterday and it hasn't let up since.

"What do you mean the police won't help you?" Lord asks, trying to make sense of what she's telling him.

Through a crackling phoneline, he's been able to piece together that Raven is missing. The sisters went to the bar last night and stayed longer than either had planned. Wren explained that when she came out of the bathroom, Raven was gone along with her purse.

"I was on hold for more than ten minutes when I called. What kind of emergency service is that?" Wren asks rhetorically. "And when I told the cops that my sister had vanished, they asked where we were. Like she was asking for trouble being in a bar, like it was typical for her to leave the bar without telling anyone. They even asked how much we had to drink and suggested that maybe there was some type of harmless romantic liaison."

"And how much *did* you drink?" Lord asks, regretting it even as the words pass his lips.

"Probably too much to drive home," Wren admits, dismissing any accusatory tone. "But I waited at the bar for hours, just in case she came back. I stayed until it closed, so by the time I left, I was sober."

Wren had already made a mental note about the blue pickup with the offensive bull balls attached to its hitch. She remembered the plate number and reported it to police, just in case there was any sort of file on the owner. Wren can't say if the person taking the call even wrote the information down. She just found it important to note though, because the truck was no longer parked beside her car when she went to check the parking lot for her sister. It was a fleeting thought, but she wondered if someone who'd make such a grotesque statement like that on his vehicle might be the type of person to hurt someone like Raven. It was a gut feeling only, but it was enough that it caused Wren to mention this detail to the police.

Wren tells Lord that she drove on the shoulder of the short highway back to the farmhouse in the valley.

"I wasn't going more than forty kilometres. Makes it easier to see something when the speed is lower. I thought maybe she decided to walk because the night was so warm. We didn't even have a breeze last night."

Wren didn't see anyone walking on the shoulder nor in the ditch. She doubled back and checked the streets in town, and then took a walk along the shoreline. By this time, the first light of day was appearing across the horizon and except for songbirds, everything was quiet. There was no traffic, no voices. The leaves on the trees didn't move and even the lake was still.

"I didn't sleep a wink," Wren continues. "And then first thing this morning, I got on my bike and rode along the grid roads nearby."

Wren neglects to tell Lord that she hit a pothole while out searching and riding. She lost balance and it caused her to swerve severely and crash into a tree. She wasn't wearing a helmet, and when she awoke from unconsciousness later in the ditch, alone with the sound of crickets and wind, she felt dried blood on her scalp and hair. She was also dizzy and disoriented, and figured she must have been knocked out for some time. Wren has no memory of riding her bike out near the lagoon.

"I stopped in at the gas station as soon as it opened," she tells Lord, "because as you know, if anything went down overnight that would be the first place where locals would be talking. But no one had heard a thing."

Wren tells him she didn't know what else to do but to call 911. Her heart broke when the police offered no help. That's when Wren began sobbing over the phone.

"They told me it isn't an emergency because Raven is not a child. The dispatcher even scolded me saying police don't usually get involved in missing persons cases until at least twenty-four hours have passed. But I know something is wrong. I have real worries and there is no timeline. Why would they dismiss me like this?"

"So what are they doing now?" Lord asks. He can't figure out how to comfort his wife over the telephone, and it makes him feel guilty, like he should have stayed home instead of going on this business trip. He knew how much it meant to Wren that her twin would be visiting, but he also wanted to give them some time alone to reconnect.

"The dispatcher says they'll send someone out later today to take a statement. In the meantime, I don't know what to do. I've called Raven's cell about a hundred times but it keeps going to voicemail. I'm worried, Lord. It isn't like her to just leave me."

"I will fly home as soon as I can find a way back to the Calgary airport," he volunteers, even though the inclement weather in the mountains has meant his business trip will be extended by at least a couple more days. He knows his suggestion to come home early leaves him at risk for losing this contract, especially if he leaves now.

"No." It's like Wren has read his thoughts. "You stay and finish. I'll be okay. Maybe the police are right," she says. "Maybe Raven just decided to go to a bonfire off the beaten path. Maybe at the Shithole, like we used to go to when we were teens. Maybe she started out there and will come back to the farmhouse smiling later today. I have to believe everything is going to be alright."

The Shithole is what the local kids call a wooded area above the outdoor skating rink in the centre of town. There are no houses there, only a quiet gully where youth built a firepit and drink beer or smoke away from judgemental eyes. They sit on old abandoned car seats that were dragged in from the dump. It happens most weekends, and mostly it's innocent and safe.

As Wren hangs up, she decides to make a few other calls to neigh-bours and friends in the vicinity. The more eyes, the better. They might be able to help her and if there's any clue as to what happened to Raven, they'll know where to look.

The first to arrive are the boys from down the road. They bring with them another cord of firewood which they unload and begin stacking beside Wren's studio before she's even able to offer them some coffee.

"Miss Raven has gone missing you say? How horrible." The broth-ers offer to walk the creek bed that runs toward the lake. "We'll walk the bike path, too, all the way back to town and we'll double our way back through the ditch to your home, Miss," says one.

It's what they say next that makes Wren want to shout out in objec-tion, and makes her heart sink. They tell her that dozens of volun-teers gathered earlier this morning to start collecting trash along the highway for the annual community cleanup. Every piece of litter, or anything that isn't part of the land, would wind up bagged and taken to the dump, including any clues that could shed light on Raven's dis-appearance. Cleaned up and sanitized, like nothing is amiss.

# FACING TRUTHS

Wren has never truly been alone. That's the reality of being a twin. They share the same birth story. Even through her pain today, Wren smiles when she thinks about how Raven would boast about being the "older" of the two. They were born eleven minutes apart.

In Raven, Wren had a loving playmate as a child and a precious confidante as a youth. They shared the same heart of spiritual connectedness but Wren is losing hope. It's been days since the annual highway cleanup, since Raven disappeared, and nothing has come to light. The RCMP have nothing to add to the missing person's report.

Raven has vanished, and even though dozens of volunteers from the town and surrounding farms have gathered as part of a search party, not one piece of evidence has surfaced. Friends and neighbours have scoured the pathway along the valley for miles, from the old Valeport meeting area all the way to Kinookimaw. A group of young girls walked the entire distance from the start of Highway 54 to the Highway 11 junction, finding nothing but old Tim Hortons coffee cups or discarded cigarette packs. Others got on bicycles to comb grid roads within a twenty-mile radius of the area, and boaters kept an eye on the shoreline, but nothing has progressed—nothing except the deepening of Wren's sadness.

She's lost a baby and now Raven is missing, too.

The RCMP made so little effort toward an active search. Wren still can't believe the explanation she was given, that "maybe she ran off with a new love interest."

"Happens all the time," they'd said. "They usually show up later filled with excuses and a bad reputation." *Assholes*, thought Wren.

Wren knows that is not her sister. Raven is meticulous, not the type to ignore phone calls and certainly not one to cause others worry by not letting them know where she is. The only thing Wren has left is faith and prayer. She speaks to her kohkum often, seeking clarity and guidance. She asks for help from the Little People, those invisible spirit helpers, those guardian angels. She prays and wants to believe that everything will turn out well, but her hope is faltering.

Wren has stopped eating. It's gotten to the point where Lord prepares food and sits with her, sometimes even feeding her just to make sure her body is nourished. Neighbours from the surrounding area do the same, bringing Wren homemade tourtière pies and smoked lake fish, just so they can have peace of mind that she's ingesting something other than despair. It has been on everyone's mind, and is the talk on coffee row each morning.

"That poor girl. I remember seeing her on the pathway with her bike almost every summer day when she was just a youngster," Wren hears from neighbours over and over again. "I sure hope they find her."

Raven's disappearance was even mentioned and prayed for in the church during Sunday services. "Dear God," they'd prayed. "Please keep this woman safe and help lead us to her whereabouts. We leave it in your loving hands. Amen."

A story and photo were posted in the local newspaper, providing a reward for information leading to any details about what might have happened. Lord put the reward money in a trust fund the moment he returned home. Ten thousand dollars, a nice sum for just providing information, but still no answers.

Quickly, the days turn to weeks, then months. What police originally suggested—that Raven left voluntarily on a pleasure excursion—can't be true. Neither her credit card nor her bank card have been used since that night at the bar.

Wren can't sleep properly. Her baby left, her sister, has disappeared—she doesn't even want to close her eyes. Every time she does, an image appears of her sister dressed in a flowing black chiffon dress that billows in the wind. Fingers of the warm summer breeze catch the tips of her hair as well, in slow motion, like the wings of a bird soaring in an updraft. Wren sometimes thinks about the baby, too, continuing to hope, but wondering if Raven is holding that little one now. *Have you gone to the same place?* Wren sobs at the very thought.

There won't be another baby anytime soon. Wren has stopped allowing her husband to touch her in an intimate way. It's just too painful to allow herself any type of joy. Instead, she stares out the kitchen window each morning, watching the brake lights on Lord's vehicle as he leaves for his office in the city. She sends him with coffee in a to-go mug that she crafted in her pottery studio, but neither the coffee nor the mug is made with love. That was the essential ingredient for everything she did, but no more. She can't find the strength to shake the grief. What used to make her happy has been replaced with nothing but grey.

Autumn arrives. The leaves slowly change and fall to the ground. Many weeks have passed with no word from or about Raven. Wren can't help but think that once the trees become bare, her surroundings will finally match the state of her soul. She begins to wail. For the first time in her life, Wren is forced to walk alone. Her twin, the one who has been with her since conception, is gone and no one knows what happened. The light of hope that exists in her heart is dimming.

# WHITE WINTER

Winter has arrived early. A soft snowfall covers the valley but does nothing to cleanse Wren's spirit. She cannot shake her pain. *How could something so bad happen to someone so good? Where is Raven?* Wren walks and walks each day. It's good exercise, though the activity is a reminder of those thousands of times that she walked with her sister up this bluff to gaze at the view from the top of the hill. By the time she returns to the farmhouse she is dripping, not with sweat but with tears she cannot seem to stop.

Wren finds herself unmotivated to do much of anything. She has lost her baby, lost her sister, and is now in jeopardy of losing her husband if she doesn't get things together soon.

Three cords of wood are stacked, without a purpose, near the new outdoor kiln that Lord built months ago. Wren hasn't been creating anything with her hands. She no longer cooks or bakes. She doesn't clean the house. She hasn't touched clay or paint. Today, there's nothing on her mind but worry and despair, and it's affecting her marriage. Lord has been supportive through it all, but still Wren worries.

Guilt is her constant companion. Every day, all she's able to do is set the coffee for the morning then sit in the living room and wait. A hard but beautifully carved piece of furniture props her up as she stares out the window. Every morning, she is greeted by a dawn filled with questions and misery. *Why did we go to bar that night? Why didn't I stay with Raven? What could I have done?* These are the queries she tortures herself with dozens of times every day. Always, there are no answers.

She no longer brushes her hair, just pulls it back into a ponytail each morning before managing to pull on the same ragged sweatshirt.

It's worn and old, a gift from Raven during their last year of high school—gold coloured, with an embroidered butterfly spreading its colourful wings. The sweatshirt brings her comfort, keeping her sister near in some way. She wears it as comfortably as an old memory.

Unanswered questions swirl around her head: *Where did Raven go? Why have the police done nothing?.* Wren thinks of the constable's words: "The security camera in the bar the night Raven disappeared did not pick up any clues." A bouquet of hillbilly helium balloons obscured any footage that could have helped.

She hardly bathes anymore, even though soaking in a hot bath in her clawfoot tub used to calm her. Now, she can't imagine enjoying even the simplest of luxuries.

Wren gets up, walking mindlessly around the house. Her thoughts go to a happy scene, even if it exists only as a wish. She imagines her sister holding her baby, kissing her and cradling the infant in her arms, as gently as someone would observe a Fabergé egg. By the time her reverie comes to an end, Wren finds she is no longer in the farmhouse but in her studio. She stares at the pottery piece she created from the remains of the fetus, and in this moment, something in Wren snaps like an elastic band stretched too far and nothing can ever be the same again. Throughout the winter, Wren's heart breaks every time she sees or hears a raven squawking.

Wren's thoughts turn to her husband, how much she absolutely loves him. She feels she is somehow committing acts of betrayal since she hasn't let him touch her intimately in such a long time. Intimacy unearths bad memories, one in particular that she'd tried to forget. As she lies in bed each night, her husband tossing beside her, Wren can't help but recall the man she first loved. Not "love" at all in retrospect, only someone who always called her *baby*, a generic term to mask that he couldn't remember whom he was sleeping with.

Wren remembers the afternoon it happened, during her college years while her first-year university dorm-mate was away. Her boyfriend came over earlier than usual. Wren was feeling ill that day, but that didn't stop him from locking the bedroom door behind him and hissing, "You're going to get some of this," while pulling out his erect penis. The man who called her *baby* violently entered Wren from behind. He grabbed her long hair the way a person holds a horse's mane. She begged him to stop, begged him to stop hurting her. That's when he slapped her on the side of the head so hard she thought blood would start dripping from her nose. He called her a *bitch* and a *slut* and told her she deserved nothing but a good boning.

When he finished, he pulled on his pants and left, leaving her in pain, bleeding, bruised and traumatized. Wren never saw him again. She never wanted to and vowed that if she ever ran into the bastard, he'd experience the same violation he'd inflicted on her. She vowed. That's where she thought she'd left the memory, but it had now come back. Some things long buried can resurface and haunt.

# ADVICE FROM A FRIEND

It is another Saturday morning and Wren's husband is doing the best he can to try and help his wife walk through her pain and move forward. He misses the smile and vibrant spirit of the woman he married, the woman who dances in the kitchen. Lord has cooked breakfast this morning: scrambled eggs and toast that he delivers on a platter to their bed, along with some advice.

"You need to start creating again," he tells her. "You haven't even used the new kiln I built for you and that worries me. You were so excited about it when we started building."

Wren abruptly replies, "I need to tell you something, Lord." She finally tells her husband that not only has she carried the heartbreak of Raven's disappearance, she has also been coping with the loss of a baby. Their baby.

"I didn't tell you because I thought you might reject me if you knew I wasn't capable of carrying a child," she sobs. Lord holds her tightly while she tries to explain further. "And I didn't want to tell you about the pregnancy because everyone knows the first three months are the crucial months, but baby left me after only two and a half months. It happened late one night while you were sleeping."

Wren wipes the tears from her face but she can't look into her husband's eyes, afraid they are too sad. He squeezes her tighter.

"Not your fault, my love. You had your reasons for wanting to keep the news to yourself. And then, Raven's disappearance. I love you and you've been through too much." Lord holds his wife and absorbs what she's just told him. They lost a baby. He begins to weep and pulls his wife even closer. Wren buries her head in his chest.

"We can try again," he promises. "We will try again."

Lord feels guilt about the Magras family curse, or at least what he was told was a curse. *No one can pass this threshold. They might carry disease.* An irrational thought passes through his mind: *Could the curse have caused the miscarriage?* He spent his whole childhood without friendship and new experiences. He never had a sleepover or a movie night with friends. No hot dog roasts around a campfire in the backyard.

Lord goes downstairs to the kitchen to fetch two Perrier waters. *This cannot be the reason why Raven disappeared. This cannot be the reason my wife worries she is infertile, why our child has gone away.* Lord sobs into his hands, which he wipes on a tea towel before bringing the water upstairs to his distraught wife.

Lord gives thanks that the curse didn't apply to his wife. He's been allowed to let Wren into his life and over the threshold into his heart. Before handing her the glass of water, Lord holds her again, as tightly as he can.

"I love you so much," he says. The couple sits in silence. Then, "You need to start creating again."

At this point, Wren cannot bring herself to admit that she incorporated the baby's remains into the last pottery piece that she did fire. It's a beautiful flower vase that now sits where that wretched photo of his dead mother used to be displayed. Late one restless night, Wren moved the photo from the mantel into a rarely used spare room at the far end of the farmhouse. That upstairs bedroom was used as a guest room, even when Wren was a girl. She looked around the room for a suitable spot.

*But who wants to share space with a dead woman in a coffin?* Wren hid the photo away, deep in a dresser drawer where no one could see it—out of sight and out of mind. Lord didn't seem to notice the displacement of the photo. Or at the very least, he didn't mention that it was no longer prominent on the mantel in the family room. When Wren had buried the photo in the drawer, she thought of Lord's description of his childhood, about the Magras curse, about how no one could pass the threshold. *Could it have migrated here with the photo, to her childhood farmhouse?*

❋　❋　❋

"I will start working again, my dear Lord," she promises.

"Maybe you can start by doing some volunteer work. It's unpaid but I think it might help you move forward," Lord suggests. Lord tells her about a project his firm is working on: an outdoor play space in an abandoned lot behind one of the downtown women's shelters.

"The kids who stay there need to have a safe space to play so we're designing a greenspace constructed with mostly recycled materials. Some of them need someone to look after them while we're doing the work."

Wren knows that since Raven disappeared, she's doing nothing more than filling up space. One day just seems to blend into the next and some days it's an ordeal for Wren just to get out of bed. What her husband is suggesting now means she'll be creating something with a purpose again, something that will witness the joy and laughter of children, and that's a good start.

"It is too quiet here with nothing but my thoughts," Wren responds, "and I do like to be around children."

"My firm will even throw in for the cost of materials if you choose to do something .. perhaps teach the kids pottery."

Lord can see the idea resonates with his wife. He also knows it's good medicine for her broken heart. His, too. He's always wanted a family, but things happen, he realizes, and neither he nor his wife are responsible for the common reality that not all babies are carried to term. This one went away. They will try again, when times are not so turbulent. The sun will shine again.

"I'll do it," Wren proclaims. "I will fire those children's work in my outdoor kiln." Then turning to Lord she says, "These sweatpants need to be thrown in the wash. Want to help me take them off?"

# LOVE LIFT ME UP

"It will make Mommy so happy to see this!"

Little Jeremy Lafond can't hide his delight as he puts the finishing touches on his pinch pottery, a technique that doesn't require throwing clay on a wheel. There is no wheel here. Only children and loads of loose clay in a box. It warms Wren's heart to see Jeremy has picked up the material and has taken to moulding it, like hugging an old friend.

Lord's firm came through. It supplied boxes of clay and other materials necessary for the creation of pottery. Wren calls it an "unpaid residency" when people in town ask what she's up to these days.

Wren notices that Jeremy is missing a tooth, which is not surprising. That's something that happens to six year-olds. His mother, though, is also missing a tooth but not because she's shedding baby teeth. Her tooth was loosened when she was punched in the face by her boyfriend. It was so badly damaged that it had to be removed. Stella and Jeremy have been living in the women's shelter ever since.

No one ever brings up the topic of Raven's disappearance anymore. They're probably uncomfortable that Wren would burst out crying whenever they'd inquire. However, the tragedy did result in changes within the community. A night-watch walk made up of volunteers has been organized. They patrol each Thursday, Friday and Saturday from ten at night until two in the morning. Even the local service club has revamped its policy on highway cleanup since the summer. Because of Wren and Raven, it will check with RCMP first to make sure that being a good Samaritan will never again mean clearing away potential evidence along the highway.

The local church mentions Raven in their prayers each Sunday. That part hasn't changed. Parishioners have mentioned the sisters during their services these past months, asking for resolution and healing. Wren is grateful for this as well, even though she's only ever attended services at the United Church a handful of times. She's pretty much isolated herself, finding that when she does venture out, the worry of others easily transfers to her, making her exhausted. And she already has more than enough of that on her own.

At the women's shelter, Wren is grateful to spend time bringing joy and healing to others through the creation of art. No one here knows about what happened to Raven. No one knows her sadness from losing the baby and because of that, no one asks questions or makes comments. There are only moments of joy when she shows up with a box of clay and ideas to share with the children. She experiences the clearing away of sadness, if only for fleeting bits of time. The happiness she sees in faces like Jeremy's warms Wren's heart. She watches the boy move his fingers over the clay, shaping a bowl for his mother. He traces a heart onto it. A child's love. Pure, trusting and so real she can feel it.

"I love this, Jeremy," she finds herself saying, wiping the tear that's formed on her face and replacing it with a smile. "This little heart that you have engraved on this bowl is just beautiful."

"I put the heart on it because I love Mommy. I want her to be happy again," he explains.

Wren hasn't slept properly in months and along with the suggestion that Wren do some volunteer work with children at the shelter, Lord has found a little blue pill to ensure a good night's rest. He came home two days ago with a prescription for Zopiclone—a prescription he picked up for himself—but proposed that Wren take it as well. She's been keeping him up at night as she tosses, turns, sighs and cries.

Along with the meds, there is a routine now too which she finds comforting: Lord makes them both some tea, then spoons some honey into the hot mug before delivering it to her in bed. He insists that each night before turning out the light, they share affirmations and reasons to be grateful, She finds that the ritual helps her and allows her the strength to do her work in the women's shelter, in a setting where tragic, real stories lie just around the corner. These women, these mothers like Stella, are here not by choice but because of violence and abuse. But at the shelter, their sad memories are not allowed to be buried. The abuse is acknowledged and then it is banished, held off by light and love and ways of rebuilding. Healing the heart. Restoring hope.

This is why building this pottery piece with Jeremy prompts Wren to share her own good memories of childhood, the way childhood is meant to be, filled with wonderment and magic. Wren decides to tell Jeremy a story told to her by Kohkum, the same story told to her when Wren's own first tooth fell out. "It was the end of day," Wren starts, "and we'd all been bathed and Kohkum read to my sister and me a story from a book. I love remembering how we would be cuddled in her arms, all warm under a blanket. Kohkum always made sure that our tummies were full of snacks, with dry meat and apples. That dry meat was yummy but hard to chew. And that's when my first tooth fell out."

Jeremy is eager to hear what happens next.

"I told Kohkum that I needed to put that tooth under my pillow because the tooth fairy was going to come and leave me a quarter, but Kohkum told me, 'No, that's not what happens.' So she told me about the Little People."

Wren goes on to describe that the Little People are invisible spirit helpers in the Cree culture. "Kind of like guardian angels I suppose. We can't actually see them, but we know they're always around." She tells Jeremy that the Little People will come during the night, take his tooth and will offer up his tooth to the universe.

"And that's when magic happens," Wren continues to Jeremy, who is listening so intently he's abandoned his pinch pot of clay altogether. "That tooth ends up where it's needed. Instead of under the pillow, it goes to a baby who can only drink milk from a bottle. No more bland formula for some special baby, Jeremy, because you gave up your tooth. And now you are part of the magic, too. Good for you."

Wren tells the boy that soon some toothless infant can enjoy peanut butter and jam sandwiches too because of him. "And that is why the Little People leave a gift. Because you gave up your tooth so that a baby can start eating peanut butter and jam sandwiches!" she finishes.

Wren feels good she passed down a story. Whether it is real or not is irrelevant, the message is there: Believe in goodness and spirit. Before Wren leaves the shelter that night, she makes sure to tell the staff to leave a loonie under Jeremy's pillow. She goes to the corner store, returning with a Kinder Surprise treat that she instructs the staff to leave on Jeremy's bedside table.

# DRIVING HOME

A deer runs out in front of Wren's car as she enters the valley near Lumsden on her way home. That's when she also sees a coyote standing at the junction where Highway 11 meets the turn off to Highway 54 and the turnoff to Wren's home in the valley. As she slows to make the turn, Wren decides to open her window and toss out the last bit of a peanut butter and jam sandwich that little Jeremy insisted he make her for her trip home. *Can't waste food,* she remembers Kohkum saying, and leaving an offering for wildlife is not wasting.

The sun disappeared from the skyline hours ago. Now is a time of twilight when moose and deer wander, sometimes even onto the highway. Wren says a prayer to the universe that those four-leggeds stay in the fields tonight, away from traffic and out of harm's way. As she opens the passenger-side window to throw out what's left of her sandwich, she hears a noise: the loud cackle of a raven. It is curious to Wren because she knows that ravens aren't supposed to fly at night. She wonders why this one is here, what it's trying to tell her.

Ten minutes later, Wren finds herself home, unloading the pinched pottery pieces made by the children. They makes her smile. The pieces will need glazing and firing in the kiln before being offered as gifts. Wren can't help but remember Jeremy's words as she takes his piece from the hatchback of her car: *My dad hurt my mom and that's why we are living here now.*

Wren couldn't stop herself from wanting to know more, so she asked staff at the shelter about Stella and why she and her son ended up there. They told her they couldn't divulge that type of information, but one young worker gave her a name when they were alone in the kitchen: the name of the person responsible for beating Jeremy's mom.

"Billy Vespas is in construction. He's started his own company. He makes a lot of money. He's the one who beat Stella."

Billy Vespas. Jeremy's dad. The name of the person who caused harm to little Jeremy and his mom. Billy Vespas. He's the one who punched Stella in the face so hard her tooth needed to be removed by a dentist. He's the one who left bruising to her cheek.

Billy Vespas.

This is a name Wren knows and hates. The memories play in her mind's eye—he is the one who violently raped her in college. She knows that *hate* is a strong word filled with nothing but darkness, but that is where this man's memory resides.

Since Raven's disappearance, Wren has been thinking about all the things that went wrong in her life. Getting involved with Billy is one of them. The memory of what he did to her has been keeping her awake at night. Billy. He hurt her in ways that left her so filled with shame she's never been able to tell anyone but Raven, her beautiful sister who always held—and honoured—Wren's secrets.

Billy. Their relationship started pleasantly enough. They met in an economics class about the *business* of art in addition to the *creation* of art. It was tedious study except for the wandering glances of another student: Billy Vespas, handsome and charming. Wren remembers the first time he asked her out after class for a cup of coffee.

He was so kind at first. Opening doors for her, insisting that he carry her backpack filled with books. He never let her pay for anything either. He'd pick up the tab at the university cafeteria as they talked for hours about how each had plans for rebuilding the future, how women are at the heart of it all. Through their discussions, Wren learned Billy had grown up with a single-parent mom as well. They became close, they shared something special.

Then came that horrible violation, and all that intimacy meant nothing. Billy was drunk when he did it. "You dirty squaws," Wren remembers him slurring. "Good for nothing but a quick fuck."

Billy Vespas. The same despicable ass who raped Wren all those years ago is the reason why a little boy and his mother are hiding in a shelter. She wants to make sure that Billy never punches out the teeth of a woman again; that he never terrorizes a little boy. "Billy Vespas," she says under her breath. "You will do no harm, no more."

The children's pottery is before her so her thoughts briefly shift to the practical, about what she needs to do in the morning to fire up her kiln and complete the children's works.

※　※　※

As is so often the case, Lord is not home. He left Wren a voice message on the answering machine saying a project deadline had been pushed up and he'd be working late at the office. He would be coming home but not till after dark. As Wren finishes washing her face, she notices Lord's vials of medication in the bathroom cabinet: insulin for his diabetes. She's watched him inject the fluid around his midriff many times. Healthy bodies produce insulin appropriately for balancing the body's sugar levels, but too much can lead to a coma or even death. As she studies it, Wren recalls a story she recently saw on the news about a nurse in Ontario who went on a killing spree at the care home where she worked. She injected residents with drugs that made their hearts stop.

Instead of going to bed, Wren reapplies her makeup, changes into a provocative dress and decides to head back to the city. If she knows anything about her husband's work ethic, he'll likely be home close to midnight. In her mind, she maps out the bars where she thinks Billy Vespas might be: places he hung out in college and probably still frequents. She figures his habits haven't changed much since she knew him.

Wren gets back into her car to drive to the city but as she rounds the corner of the long driveway leading to the main highway, something stops her. She thinks she sees a woman standing in the moonlight near the creek that runs past the ditch. *Raven?*

Moonlight can play tricks on the eyes and the imagination. As she strains to look again, she sees only bulrushes, a bunch of fence posts donning old footwear and a lone coyote. His eyes reflect off her headlights like patio lanterns. It's enough to make Wren change her plans, however. The sudden invocation of Raven prompts Wren to rethink her evening's agenda. She puts the car in reverse and slowly pulls back into the farmhouse driveway.

What will happen to Billy can wait.

# ELEMENTS

"So you around next week, Lord?" Wren asks her husband.

Lord is rarely at home these days. They're at the table eating raisin-bread toast.

"I'm almost finished up with that project in Alberta. But I have to head out again tomorrow. I think I will drive this time. After this, hopefully I'll be at home more often. I'll probably be gone all of next week." Lord takes another bite of his breakfast and inquires, "Why do you ask?"

"It's been a while since we've taken a trip anywhere," laments Wren.

"You're right, my love." Lord's expression changes from sleepy to intrigued. "Any place you want to go in particular?"

Wren tells him she wants to go somewhere hot. Maybe Cuba.

"That is an excellent idea. I'll check out some travel agents while in the city today and bring home some brochures. Look at the time," he says, and quickly finishes up his last bite. "I'll see you for dinner. And, don't worry about cooking me anything. I'll pick up something to go."

Not five minutes later, Wren watches her husband's car make the turn from their grid road onto the main highway. He's got plans for the day and so does she.

It has not been difficult to stalk Billy, not hard to figure out his routine at all. Wren found him right away online. He works as an independent roofer and has ads around town. His truck dons the logo for his company and his contact information.

After Lord leaves for the office each day, Wren leaves for the city. She's been following Billy for the past three days. His schedule is the same every morning. At 8:30 he visits a local Tim Hortons on North Albert Street. He doesn't use the drive-thru because it's often faster to use the counter service, so he orders inside. She even knows what he gets: oatmeal with milk and an extra-large double-double coffee to go. She has sat, watched and noted everything, from what he wears to his mannerisms.

This morning and before leaving for the city, her plan is to alter her appearance as much as possible, tie her hair up in a bun and hide it under a hat. She practises changing her speaking voice, with a slight French accent.

Wren arrives at the Tim Hortons parking lot before Billy does. It's 8:27 a.m. As she watches Billy's truck pull into a space beside her car, her breathing increases just a bit. She's suddenly nervous about whether she can pull this off, and is hoping he doesn't recognize her.

It's been a decade since she last saw him. She prays he won't remember. By sheer willpower, Wren stops her hands from shaking. It's showtime. Her plan is to approach him, not confront him, but just meet him head-on, be polite. Kill him with kindness as it were.

"Oh, hello," she says as he exits his truck. "I notice you do roofing. I've seen your truck here a couple of mornings now when I've stopped in for a tea." Her French accent is iffy, though only a Francophone would detect this.

"Morning, ma'am." Billy's greeting is jovial, and it's clear to Wren that he does not recognize her.

"I don't know if you take jobs out of town," she tells him, "but part of my roof needs some work. More so now that the weather has come in. I don't want any further damage." She tells him that the person she'd contracted earlier in the fall had some health problems so wasn't even able to start the job and she doesn't want to chance leaving the work until springtime. "Could you do an estimate? If you take out-of-town jobs that is."

The two chat for a short while and Billy offers to come out to the farmhouse the next day.

"That won't work, I have to head out of town for a few days for work. But on Monday I will be at home." That's the day Lord indicated he'll be out of province.

Billy checks the work schedule on his cellphone. "I seem to be available Monday," he says. "What's the address?"

"It is a bit of a maze to get to my house, so I won't give you farmer's directions." Billy gives a slight laugh at Wren's comment because he's been in southern Saskatchewan and gotten lost on the grids. Rural people know about the red barn by the slough where you're supposed to turn left toward the Baker's farm, whoever Baker is, and then make a right where there's a fork in the road, marked only by an abandoned postbox. It's rural lingo and farmer's directions, understood and followed by the local folk.

"I'll draw you a map," Wren offers.

She doesn't want to leave any type of electronic trail, so she jots down crude directions on the back of a pamphlet. She makes sure to keep her red leather gloves on while drawing — no fingerprints to leave behind. When Billy asks her for a phone number "in case there is a change of plans," Wren writes down the number for a disposable cellphone she purchased recently for exactly this purpose.

"So, Monday, then," she says and thanks him. "I'll make sure to put the coffee on before you show up, then you can look at what's needed and let me know if you can do this job. Lord knows I don't want to go through my first blizzard without having it fixed. I swear, I saw a couple of shingles blow right off with that strong wind from the north the other day."

Billy folds the pamphlet with the directions, slides it into his back pocket and heads to the coffee shop. Wren doesn't follow him inside to order a tea. Instead, she feigns having to make a phone call. She waits for him to go in through the door and gets back into her vehicle, driving out of the parking lot feeling satisfied with herself. Contact has been made. A plausible trap has been set, which will soon lure Billy's wretched soul to his doom.

Wren thinks about Stella and Jeremy as she makes the righthand turn back toward busy North Albert Street. Then she mutters the words, "You will take no more, Vespas."

# GOD'S WILL

A few days after Lord leaves for business in Alberta, Wren is standing at the bathroom mirror, staring at her reflection. She notices a wrinkle between her eyebrows. She notices that she has no smile lines, but creases have formed in a downward direction at the sides of her mouth, frownlines indicating prolonged sadness. She stares intently, examining her face.

In that moment she has thoughts of vengeance again, then realizes that the feeling is a natural part of grieving or experiencing injustice. *Even God does it,* she assures herself, remembering stories from the Bible, including one told to her by her beloved kohkum. According to the Exodus account, Moses held out his staff and the Red Sea was parted by God. The Israelites walked on the exposed dry ground and crossed the sea, followed by the Egyptian army. Moses lowered his staff once the Israelites had crossed and the sea closed up, drowning the entire Egyptian army.

It's a Bible passage that will always stay with Wren. She remembers it from her childhood when she and Raven would cuddle on the couch with Kohkum. They'd have a plate of sugar cookies in front of them, baked with love, and they'd watch *The Ten Commandments* with Charlton Heston playing the role of Moses. Along with other feature films, that movie was always on television, always a part of the Christmas season. Not too many weeks from now, it'll be Christmas again. But without the movie, without Kohkum, without her Raven.

*If God can decree that some people need to be put to death, then am I doing anything wrong if I do the same?* Wren asks herself, remembering that stern punishment has always been a part of her culture as well.

She recalls a story that her kohkum used to tell when the girls misbehaved. Kohkum told the story as a lesson to always be mindful about how we treat others, that bad deeds do not go unnoticed, that doing good will be rewarded, and if we cause harm, it will be met with the same.

Kohkum's story centres around a group of bad young men. She called them the Young Dogs. They were a group of wayward youth who had been banished from their Cree and Nakota tribes because each had committed crimes too unspeakable for a young girl's ears. Kohkum didn't go into details about how the Young Dogs brutalized Elders and those who were two-spirited, nor how they sexually molested many, even children. They were poisonous, and poison needs to be removed, so each was banished and forced to leave the safety of the tipi villages to set out on their own.

So these wandering and ostracized young men found each other in the bush. They banded up and travelled together, raiding what they could from nearby camps when the night would fall. They would capture women, taking them hostage and using them as sex slaves. That's how the story is always told.

On a clear summer's night, one young woman managed to escape, hiding amongst reeds at the edge of the lake where the Young Dogs had set up camp. It's at this time that Creator sent a fire from heaven. Thunder and the most violent lightning storm touched the ground with vengeance, burning up each of the Young Dogs and the tents they had been sleeping in, leaving only dark patches of burned-up grass in their places. The lightning struck only in one part of the valley that night and disappeared as quickly as it arrived. The young woman hiding in the reeds was spared—the only one left alive. When all was quiet, she ran back to the safety of her family and the encampment a few miles away. This story has been handed down since the middle of the nineteenth century, a time before the white man settled in the valley.

*Creator has rid the world of filth and danger many times*, Wren tells herself. She checks her reflection in the mirror. She makes no attempt to wipe away the tear that rolls, ever so slowly, down her right cheek as she thinks of Raven. Later this morning, Billy will be arriving as planned to check out the roof, or so he thinks.

It's almost eleven, the scheduled time for Billy's appointment at the farmhouse. Wren looks out the kitchen window toward the grid road to see if his roofing vehicle might be coming down the long and winding driveway. It is.

During these passing moments, Wren remembers her prayer to Kohkum last night asking for advice about her coming plans. She didn't dream of a scarecrow but was instead awakened during the early-morning hours by the sounds of something rustling outside. When she glanced out the window, Wren saw a deer. It was a white-tailed buck with a magnificent set of horns digging under the snow-fall and looking for nourishment.

Wren needs nourishment, too. For her soul. She's been reading the Bible over these last weeks looking for answers. *An eye for an eye* and all that. The Ten Commandments. She knows the Bible condemns killing but in her mind, Wren doesn't see this as killing. It's more like silencing a bad noise, like the Red Sea when it swallowed up a whole army, like fire from the heavens that burned a village of Young Dog ne'er-do-wells who only caused pain and suffering. Evil must be destroyed.

But the time for pondering has come to an end. Billy Vespas has abused women—her, Stella and who knows how many others since she last saw him. *How much harm and evil has he inflicted upon this world?* Wren wonders as she hears a truck driving up and then its door slam shut.

She checks the mirror again. This time she sees not her own reflection, but the eyes of a mother bear.

# FAIRIES

Wren has always wondered about magic and other worlds. As a child, she saw specks of light along the landscape when she'd wake up during the night to get a glass of water. Kohkum always told her, "They are fireflies," but to little Wren, those lights belonged to fairies. Maybe even to Little People reminding her that they would always stay close, protecting her from harm.

The forecast says there is mild weather for the rest of the week but Wren wants it to snow. She wants to see those large flakes fall and cover her tracks. Cover her plan. Her Red Sea parting. Wren has asked the fairies for help today. She's asked them before and they always come through. *Let it snow.* As Wren hears Billy knock on the door, tiny snowflakes begin to fall from the sky.

"So glad you could make it," she says while hiding three small blue pills in her cardigan sweater pocket, "Come on in. Coffee is on."

The thing about Zopiclone is that it can leave an aftertaste, so Wren talks about her apiary and how the bees this year seem to have been attracted to alfalfa instead of other types of wildflowers.

"Because of all that, the honey in your latte will have a distinct flavour."

Wren doesn't use the regular coffee maker, but instead uses the espresso machine, one of the only things that Lord brought into the farmhouse from his previous home. He likes that the machine can produce a froth of milk stacked as high as meringue on a pie.

"It's good," Billy says. "I didn't know you were a beekeeper. That's cool."

Wren makes small talk with Billy for the next half an hour, waiting for the sleeping pill to take hold and for her plan to take flight. She glances out the window at the falling snow: fresh, white and falling steadily. Wren understands it as a sign that she's on the right path, that what she's about to do will be muted and covered. Like it never happened.

"So, I noticed your shingles," Billy says, his speech beginning to slur a bit. "They look in good shape to me, but there's no harm in being sure." He sets down a brochure that outlines quotes for various roofing projects.

"Muffin?" asks Wren, extending a freshly baked plate of baking laced with more Zopiclone. "I have butter if you want. Here."

Billy eagerly takes one of the drug-laced muffins. There's no more need for small talk. He hurriedly eats the baked treat and passes out right at the kitchen island. He falls off his stool to the floor with a thud. Wren slaps him across the face, hard, to make sure he's no longer conscious, no longer aware of what's happening. When she's sure he's out cold, she ascends the stairs to grab vials of her husband's insulin.

Wren returns to the kitchen seconds later and fills up a syringe. She removes the boot and sock from Billy's left foot, not an easy task when someone is a dead weight on the floor, unmoving. She slips the needle between his toes and presses the clear liquid in deep. The excess insulin in his system will stop his heart soon. She gives him a second injection between another pair of toes. "Just to make sure," she mutters, knowing Billy will be dead soon.

Wren takes a sip of her coffee and heads outside. She gazes peacefully at the rolling pasture, the rustling leaves in the trees, the delicate flakes of snow falling on everything. She will add wood to her outdoor kiln soon. She'll turn Billy's bones to ash.

# ASHES

Wren lives in the valley. Her old farmhouse is tucked away between several buttes and far out of sight from the main highway. There are no other homes in any direction for miles. There was no one to witness Billy's death, just as there was no one to witness Raven's disappearance. Wren generously feeds the kiln with the birch a neighbour down the road supplied earlier in the year. Billy's body is heavier than Wren ever imagined and she has a hell of time dragging his corpse outside from her kitchen floor. Wren decides she will use the ashes from Billy's burned bones to make a vessel for kitchen utensils, like potato mashers or spaghetti spacers.

"For once, you will provide something useful," she utters to the skin and bones. Wren's disassociates herself, imagining she's dragging nothing more than a heavy load of dirty laundry stuffed into a duffel bag. She removes the cowboy boot from his other foot to hang on her fence. She decides to paint the boot a hue of fluorescent pink before displaying it. *Or maybe rainbow colours,* she thinks and laughs. *But what about the roofing vehicle?* The lake is frozen. Not thick but frozen.

"Only an idiot would drive on that ice at this time of year. Too risky. Too thin yet," Wren chirps. "Only an idiot, like this roofer from the city, would drive his truck out on the ice. A *cidiot.*" She laughs at her own joke while stoking the outdoor kiln. She'll feed the body in first then set it aflame.

Wren makes a promise to Raven as she pushes Billy's body into the cavity of brick and mortar, "If anyone has harmed you, my lovely sister, this is where they will find themselves. Please come back to me, Raven. Let me know you are unharmed." Tears stream down her face.

The body in the kiln reminds Wren of an MRI, except this one will not take photos. She'll need to stoke the fire often over the next couple of days. She'll need to feed this fire day and night. It'll take two days to burn the bones to ash, and she'll have to wait another day for the kiln to cool before she can harvest.

The smell of Billy's burning flesh doesn't bother Wren, but instead reminds her of smoked ribs, smoked turkey, smoked meat. Before Lord returns home, there will be nothing but a pile of ash in her kiln. The kiln Lord built. *Leaving only bad ash*, thinks Wren. *Now wiped from the earth and her sacred soul. The soul of all women. Bad ash. Red Sea parting. Young Dogs destroyed by fire, a riddance of filth and those who leave nothing behind but pain.*

As Billy's body slowly cooks, Wren lights a bonfire in the firepit. A place where years earlier, she sat with Kohkum and Raven and roasted marshmallows. A place where she will dance and say prayers tonight. Wren goes back into her house to fetch a portable stereo and a favourite CD: Andino Suns. She will play their rendition of "Weichafe" and set the stereo to repeat.

"Weichafe", a melody dedicated to revolution and rebuilding, to what she is doing now. Wren dances around the large blaze that has sparked in her firepit, while saying a prayer for Billy's soul. That he will harm no more. She stabs at the naked sky with the flaming end of a stick. There are no stars out tonight. There is only cloud cover and the light falling of snow. That light falling of snow. She thanks the fairies for this perfect gift.

Wren locates the keys which she took from Billy's pocket earlier. "Time for an accident," she whispers, knowing the ice on the lake will not support the weight of Billy's truck. It's too early in the winter season to be driving on the lake, especially if it's parked on a fault where the current is active. Wren has observed the lake for years. She knows and respects its power. It can and will devour.

Red Sea parting. Fire from the sky.

# THE LAKE HOLDS SECRETS

Wren has walked or biked along the pathway that runs along the lake so many times. As a child, it was where she and her sister would hike, toward what used to be called Butler's but what is now the Blue bird Café. They'd get a plate of fish and chips with the money they'd earned for doing chores at home. Wren has studied the lake during winter, spring, summer and fall. It can appear so calm and serene but underneath are deadly undercurrents where even fish don't swim. There are several of these such places, where water churns, dragging the unknowable down to murky depths from which there is no return.

Kohkum used to call it "the Edge." The place where sea monsters live; a portal where good and evil meet. Wren will drive Billy's truck there, to a spot where she knows the lake heaves, a current runs and the ice is thin. She'll leave that red roofing truck on a fault during this snowfall. The lake will swallow it up, and this world will forever be rid of Billy Vespas's violent fists. Wren can still see the faint bruising on Stella's face.

It's midnight when Wren drives Billy's truck off her property, under the cover of darkness. She made sure to clean out the truck's cab before driving away. She'll get rid of his cellphone and notepads, which could leave traces of jobs he's done recently, including coming out to see her. She'll burn them. Wren drives to the end of 16th Street in Regina Beach and turns toward the bike path at the base of the hill. There's a small opening where this truck will fit on the pathway. It's a gamble though because the path is narrow and not meant for vehicles.

"Turn to the right and make a wicked drive down the embankment," Wren mutters to herself, "and, don't hit any boulders. Shit. Get on the ice and hope not to sink before halfway on the lake where the monsters live. Billy, you're a monster. This is where you belong. This is what you deserve."

Her descent from the embankment and over the crest of rocks that line the shore way can be described as nothing less than terrifying. The rocks catch the wheels of the Ford Ranger and Wren experiences the first moments of regret that she ever dreamed up such a scheme. The front wheels seem momentarily stuck, spinning between two small boulders. The truck feels as though it will fall on its side rather than go forward onto the frozen expanse of lake toward the ice heave that beckons. Wren is in a panic. She calls on the fairies again, to whatever entities might be helping her in this task. It may have been loose gravel or her loose mindset that willed the vehicle forward, but suddenly the wheels spin out from the grip of those frozen rocks and Wren is back on the bumpy ride down the embankment and toward the frozen lake.

Wren drives a quarter-mile across the layer of ice, not knowing if it will hold the weight of the vehicle she's driving. November is too early to be on the lake. She drives with the window down and her seatbelt unbuckled in case she needs to make a quick escape. This far from the shoreline is a place where the water runs deep; a good place where secrets will be kept. A place where no one will find this abandoned vehicle. It will sink and be taken by the lake and with it, any trace of Billy. Wren stops on the fault line, puts the truck into park and steps out. She's crying, her memory of Raven's disappearance still fresh in her mind.

It occurs to Wren that what she's done is her way of yelling at the universe, of asking, *Why did this piece of shit get to live and prosper, and hurt people, and lie and still carry on as though nothing has happened?* She curses the RCMP for their inaction on Raven's disappearance. As she slams the truck door, Wren finds herself hoping that Billy's disappearance will be met with the same lack of examination. Wren wipes the tears that have fallen from her eyes with the sleeve of her coat. She takes a deep breath, inhaling the good, exhaling the bad.

Once she feels centred, she begins her walk back to the shoreline. Wren knows the falling of snow will bury that truck, cover her footprints, and erase any evidence of the crimes she's committed.

"Fairies, you have conspired. Thank you," she breathes.

Wren spots a lone coyote watching her as she exits the truck. The air is so quiet even her footsteps don't make a sound. Wren walks home along the pathway, then through the Village of Buena Vista. There are no streetlights so keeping to herself is easy. She's wearing dark clothing, helping her blend into the darkness of night and the darkness of her secret, which will soon rest at the bottom of this lake. She hopes her plan will work, and that the ice heave on the lake will break before morning, swallowing the truck.

# MEMENTO MORI

What started out as a light snowfall has turned hard and constant. School buses don't run the following morning. Wren knows this because watching the highway is part of her routine, has been since she and Lord moved back to the farmhouse. Wren pours a strong coffee each morning before her husband leaves for work. She watches the tail lights on his car as he leaves for the city. Eight-thirty in the morning. She can set her clock by it. Today though, that stretch of highway which she can see from her kitchen window is quiet. No school buses. No plows. No traffic.

Wren wonders if she'll be able to make it out of her own driveway today. She takes a sip from her big mug and walks to the other side of the house to the window that looks toward the east, where the day begins.

The smoke from Wren's kiln has been releasing all night. She's been stoking the fire since returning home from the lake. She even got up at four in the morning to add more birch. Quiet, alone, unseen. Now, finally, the flame has died leaving only embers. Wren will collect the fragments from Billy's remains tomorrow.

Wren decides to throw some clay on her wheel. It is a snow day anyway, so she might as well do something that will amount to good. It's so quiet outdoors this morning. The thick blanket of snow masks every sound, even the wind is silent. Once indoors, Wren opens a new box of clay. It's like some sort of homecoming each time she does this. The smell of fresh earth sends her a special greeting, like the clay itself is welcoming her to pick it up and start moulding.

Wren puts on an apron and gathers some slip. She turns on the potter's wheel. Its hum is always soothing: the sound of creation, reminding her of the wind. As she hunches over the wheel to coax the clay into rising, her mind drifts to times when she and Raven gathered wolf-willow seeds from the bush. Their kohkum had taught them how to pick the seeds and clean off the husk to reveal a perfect, sharp, brown seed at its core. As they removed the outer husk, there was that smell of something wild and free. They'd sit for hours, stringing the wolf-willow seeds into the shape of a necklace or bracelet. A precious memory, and Wren finds herself wishing that her sister was sitting with her now, playing with clay.

She's happy to be using her pottery wheel again: that whirl of promise that will transform a piece of Mother Earth into a form that signals rejoicing, something that has not been seen in Wren's studio for months. Not since Raven went missing. Not since her husband encouraged Wren to do pottery with the kids at the women's shelter. At least her time at the shelter allowed her to find some new kind of purpose. Getting rid of debris and things not useful. Like Billy. Wren watches the mound of clay as it spins around on the wheel.

She says a prayer to her sister: "Today, I make an image in your honour. It will tell the story of strength, and bone black will be the finish. His bones, for all the hurts we have endured but never deserved."

Crafting and moulding, Wren forms the clay as delicately as dressing a newborn child. She puts her fist in the middle of the mound and it rises. She gently glides her fingers to the outside of the vessel. It needs a lip. Something that will allow it to speak. Within the sound of silence outdoors, the sound of silence within her own heart, Wren coaxes the clay into form. It's almost noon by the time Wren finishes moulding and finessing this new piece. It'll have to sit for another day before she can fire it, along with the bone black ash that's in her outdoor kiln. Bones of Billy.

Wren looks at her long driveway. Snow covered. She'll call the neighbours down the road for a plow later. Right now, she wants to see if there is a red dot on the lake. Billy's red truck. Blood of my brother. Wren's wish is that any evidence of her nocturnal activity will be wiped clean. She hopes the fairies have danced and that lake spirits have taken this offering to rid filth from the earth.

Wren removes her apron and leaves the studio. Minutes later and a short drive down to the lakeside, Wren gazes out towards the middle of the lake. The wind throws her hair over her eyes causing her to lose focus momentarily. The sun shines brightly as the shrill voice of a bohemian waxwing sounds. It jumps from branch to branch along the aspens that grow in the valley. The bird rests in a bush, where it eats the red buffalo berries that continue to hang through the winter months. Wren takes it as a sign from her bird cousin that there will be no red for her to see on the lake today.

Last night's snow is sticky. The temperature has warmed since yesterday and the snow sticks to the bottom of Wren's boots, making her feet heavy. There are no footprints in the snow other than the ones she's making now as she walks. Thick snow lays heavy on the frozen lake as well. She glances toward the panorama and the fault line where she left the truck. Nothing. It's disappeared, fallen through the ice to rest at the bottom of a very deep lake. There is no evidence of tire tracks on the pathway, nor on the embankment where Wren almost got stuck. Nothing looks out of place; nature's canvas is wiped clean again by a blanket of fresh snow. By the fairies. Not even snowmobiles would go out on the lake this early in the season, so no tracks like that either. Only clean white flakes. Wren decides to celebrate.

"Red Sea parting, Young Dogs swallowed up," she mutters to her waxwing friend. "There are fresh cinnamon buns at the gas station. Cinnamon, the smell of comfort."

Wren returns to her vehicle parked at the end of the street, near an area bald of trees. Wren says a silent prayer for what she's done. She prays for the inner child of Billy's soul, the child who had lost his way and turned into a man who slapped and raped and punched. That innocent part of his spirit needs to be set free. Now, that part of him that was once pure will be allowed to dance with the fairies again.

Wren slowly makes the sign of the cross before putting her car in gear. A cinnamon bun awaits.

# FORGIVEN BUT NOT FORGOTTEN

By the time she gets back to her farmhouse, Wren's sweet cinnamon bun is only half-eaten. It occurs to her that while she wants to have feelings of elation, she cannot. What she's done is wrong, she knows this, even if that piece of shit deserved what he got.

Instead of returning to her studio to revisit her newly created piece of pottery, she goes instead to her bedroom and retrieves a pink rosary from her bedside table that used to belong to Kohkum. Wren feels the need to connect with her grandmother's spirit. She needs to seek guidance and validation that what she's done was what needed to be done. No more guilt. It was like putting down a rabid animal, a humane act meant mostly to protect the innocent. Billy felt no pain. He just went to sleep, a slumber from which he never awoke.

As Wren holds the rosary, she's thinks about prayer, and all the times her kohkum told her that the universe provides if you just ask. The memory brings her comfort. Sitting now at her kitchen island, Wren can see her kohkum at work baking bannock, swirling freshly picked berries in a pot to make a sweet jam. She hears her grandmother's humming and she can see her gentle smile. Innocent times of love and belonging. Kohkum's kitchen is the place where so much love was shared, and so much food to nourish body and soul. She thinks of the long walks Kohkum would take with the girls. The smell of fresh sap from trees and the lake-smell of algae carried by a warm breeze as they made their way along the valley. There was no pathway back then but it still was a stretch along the lake that was a bustle of activity, all the way from town to Valeport. There was a little cove of land that housed a dance hall, and local folks would dock their boats along the shoreline to make merry and get caught up on the latest goings-on.

That part of the valley has always been lush and remains so to this day, dotted with sloughs. It's where families gather for picnics in order to watch scads of geese and ducks nest in the area. Kohkum would always tell the twins that along those sloughs grows a large patch of sweetgrass. *It's what we pray with*, she'd often remind them. Then, the girls' grandmother would say, "When I was a little girl, we did a lot of things differently. We harvested the land. No need to head to a grocery store or drug store. Creator provides here, provides everything."

Wren can still see her kohkum setting down some tobacco while the girls ate Spam sandwiches with mustard that were packed for the hike. "I set down this tobacco," she'd say, "to thank Mother Earth, the spirit world and our Creator for bringing us such abundance." They'd sit near the marshy area alongside the lake, watch the ducks and listen to the voices of frogs.

The twins spent a lot of time at their grandma's house. Wren remembers one Saturday afternoon in early September. She knows it was September because she can see herself wearing a new pair of jeans that Kohkum had purchased for her as a back-to-school gift. Seems she'd give a gift for almost any occasion, even it wasn't a real holiday. Her grandmother believed every day was special and deserving of note. This day, Kohkum was teaching the girls how to create designs in beadwork. It's something she started teaching them back when they lost their first teeth, before they started grade one.

The memory brings a smile to Wren's face as she thinks of Kohkum giving them big jars filled with hundreds of large pony beads. While she cooked or baked, Kohkum would tell the little girls to separate the beads into groups of different colours. She'd bring out fine wool and have them string the beads according to the colours of the rainbow. Only wool; no sharp needles yet on which to prick their small fingers.

Kohkum instructed that they place three beads of each colour in a line to create a rainbow pattern: red, orange, yellow, green, blue, indigo and violet. She told them that rainbows are magical because they represent the meeting place where heaven touches the earth. The girls would practise placing the beads until a very long string of them had been created. That's when Kohkum would store their works, saving them in what she called her "treasure chest," which was a shoebox where all the precious items the girls had made for her were kept.

Later that year, Kohkum brought out those stringed pony beads to use as decoration on her Christmas tree. As the twins grew, Kohkum taught them how to thread a needle, then how to string the smaller seed beads which would eventually be fashioned into a basic necklace. Eventually, those handmade necklaces would be given away as gifts to friends and teachers at school.

The girls adored this time, learning Kohkum's teachings and sharing in her talents. When the girls were seven years old, Kohkum decided the time had come to teach them how to tack glass beads onto leather and make key chains. She told the twins, "Nosisimak, my granddaughters, go upstairs to my sewing room and retrieve the materials." They knew exactly what would be needed and ran up the big stairwell, challenging each other, "Last one is a rotten egg!"

Once in that comfortable room where Kohkum would spend hours creating beadwork, sewing quilts or piecing together rag rugs, the girls knew just where to look. Kohkum kept all her beads in an old Mackintosh toffee box. It was made of tin, and the beads made a tinkling that sounded like applause each time the box was moved from its place on the shelf. Wren had chosen pink and blue glass beads to go into her floral design. She remembers joking with Raven about how she loved having a sister, but always wanted a brother, too, and that's why she used the two colours: pink and blue.

Raven had chosen two differing hues of purple. She wanted to make a diamond design. The plan was to make gifts for their mom. Her birthday was coming up soon and Kohkum always said, "It's more special to give a gift made with your own hands than to go to some store and buy something that anyone else can buy, too."

The girls were happy to accept the challenge of adhering beads to leather as they'd watched Kohkum do hundreds of times. They looked forward to this new opportunity but before they could begin, the telephone rang downstairs, interrupting Kohkum's lesson.

Standing here now holding Kohkum's rosary, Wren remembers that sad moment. It was the first time she'd ever seen her grandmother cry. Kohkum's sobbing could be heard through the heating vent that led from the kitchen to the craft room upstairs where the girls waited. It was a sobbing that came from deep within, that the girls were not supposed to witness.

# A WOUND THAT NEEDS REOPENING

Wren knew that Kohkum was also a twin. The maternal side is where the gene comes from in a family. The girls overheard the phone conversation that broke Kohkum's heart—that her twin sister Dodi had committed suicide.

Wren has no real memories of Auntie Dodi. She didn't come around much and the girls knew of her only from photos and other people's stories. Dodi never married or had children. According to stories told in hushed tones and only ever overheard by chance or eavesdropping, Wren recalls the sad tales of how Dodi spent time in and out of rehabilitation centres. She'd even spent some time in jail.

In one of those sad anecdotes, Wren learned that Auntie Dodi had stabbed a man with a broken beer bottle. It was late in the night after an all-day house party somewhere in the city. As the story goes, a man grabbed Dodi from behind and started dry humping her. Dodi told him to stop. He didn't, so she smashed the bottle and stabbed him with the jagged edge. He didn't die, but he likely has a scar, like the scars left on Dodi from years of hatred and abuse.

Wren remembers it is was a godsend that Grandpa Tony came back to the house moments after the phone rang. He was able to comfort and settle Kohkum's grief, as he'd done so many times before. The young girls could only stand, frozen in disbelief, at the news of Dodi's death. Kohkum described to her husband how Dodi had always stood as her protector against Father Hector at the Qu'Appelle Indian Residential School. When that god-forsaken devil would corner them, it was always Dodi who stepped in, offering herself to pain and sin so that her twin sister didn't have to suffer. It wouldn't be until

years later that both Wren and Raven would come to know the full
extent of what went on in those so-called places of learning.

"He dragged her off into a broom closet so many times," Kohkum
told her husband. "After a while, she stopped whimpering when it
happened. She'd come back to our room later, sweaty and sometimes
bruised. Dodi never told me everything that happened. She never
told anyone. But something inside her broke, something that even
God could never fix."

Wren remembers Mooshum Tony holding their grandmother as
she sobbed. He held his wife as she managed to weep out the story
of how Auntie Dodi died. "The coroner says it was an overdose of
sleeping pills along with a twenty-six of vodka. Her heart stopped.
They found her in a rooming house. She was naked and had soiled the
bedsheets. Landlord sent a bill along with the ambulance attendants
who collected her. Says he wants to be reimbursed for damages."

Wren remembers her kohkum saying that Dodi had no posses-
sions except for a couple of old photos that had to be pried from her
hands. One was of Kohkum and Dodi smiling, dressed in simple
frocks and wearing white socks. It was a photo that must have been
taken when the girls were just admitted to the residential school. The
other photo was a picture of Wren and Raven. They were babies and
Dodi was holding them both, one in each arm, and posing in front of
a Christmas tree.

As the sad memory surfaces, Wren goes to the kitchen to make
herself a coffee. She is still holding Kohkum's rosary. She glances
through a newspaper she had the forethought to pick up when she
went to town for the cinnamon bun. Buried somewhere near the back
of the paper is a small article, easy to breeze past. It describes a priest,
Father Hector, now retired, an old man living in the city. His recent
court case alleging sexual abuse resulted in acquittal.

A former residential school student had brought forth allegations,
but the court found there was not enough evidence to substantiate
guilt. The old priest walks freely among men again, it would seem, and
the souls he destroyed will never know justice. Auntie Dodi was one

of them. Kohkum, too, added to the sorrow. Even though the courts did nothing to him, Father Hector had sentenced women—girls at the time—to a prison from which there would never be release. He robbed them of their spirit each time his filthy hands touched their flesh. They are the ones who are imprisoned: in their hearts, minds and down to their very souls.

Wren sets the rosary down next to the newspaper. Instead of drinking her coffee, she goes to the couch to lay down for a nap to recharge.

# LEAVE ME ALONE

A person is never supposed to go to sleep if there is something bad on one's mind. *The bad thing will follow them and cause bad dreams,* Kohkum would often advise, one of those pieces of her logic that Wren always took to heart. It's why Wren sets aside a few moments for quiet reflection each night before turning in, to offer thanks for the day and for all the blessings that have come her way. But it isn't nighttime, and Wren didn't think she'd fall asleep so quickly on the couch. She hasn't said prayers and there are bad things on her mind. Kohkum was right. Those thoughts did follow Wren into her dreams.

The dream starts with Wren falling off her bike while trying to find clues about what happened to Raven. Her dream takes her back to that time, a time in which she has no real recollections but in its replaying, Wren has blood on her head, blood all over her hands. She's panicked. Where is she? Why is she so thirsty? Then a scarecrow appears with a jug of water. Pure water, cold and clean. Wren drinks it eagerly even though there is a thread of something red running through it. Poison? Maybe, but a dying woman asks no questions, only accepts the help offered. She gulps it in.

Wren wakes from the dream momentarily, and then just as quickly closes her eyes again, exhausted. The dream continues. There is the scarecrow again, except this time it is not outdoors in the meadow; instead, it sits in the recliner next to the sofa where Wren is asleep. The scarecrow talks to her. It tells her that even though the old priest is retired, Father Hector still fondles young women. He goes to coffee row each morning at a local strip mall on the outskirts of the city. Scarecrow describes the restaurant and where it's located. Her dream is like watching a movie, detailed and vivid.

Scarecrow tells her that one of the greeters in this small business is the niece of the family that owns the diner. Renée is in her twenties and has Down syndrome. Renée's job is to greet everyone with a smile and tell them it will be just a minute before they are seated. In addition to tipping the waitress, patrons typically leave Renée a small token. Maybe a quarter, maybe a loonie.

Because Father Hector knows her routine, Scarecrow tells Wren that something evil is about to happen again. Scarecrow opens its mouth wide, showing her its jagged teeth. It continues to talk in a voice that is more rasp than coherent words, as if there is something stuck in its throat. It tells Wren that today that old pervert will follow Renée to the storage room when she goes to get more candy for the dish at the host station.

"Later today," Scarecrow predicts, "Father Hector will follow that young girl and offer to help. Once he's alone with her, he'll bring out a trinket from his right pants pocket."

Scarecrow pulls out a cheap piece of costume jewellery from the tattered apron covering its foul body. It tells Wren that the priest will give a fake pearl necklace to Renée. She will allow him to fasten the clasp around her neck. That's when he'll kiss the back of her neck, startling her. He'll tell her she is his baby. His sweetheart. *We have known each other for such a long time,* he'll say. *You have always been special to me.* Then he'll fondle her breasts under the white cardigan she's wearing. He'll leave the restaurant before Renée returns to the front desk to meet customers, gently playing with the gift of pearls.

"He's a predator who has gotten away with his crimes. Always has. Violating that girl is his way celebrating," Scarecrow hisses.

Wren wakes covered in sweat. She glances at the empty chair where the scarecrow was sitting and talking. Its new upholstery, blue and white, reminds Wren of the wind. She puts her hands to her face and begins to cry, wondering if she was just visited by some bad spirit, or worse, if she is starting to hallucinate. The stress of late has been adding up and Wren has been spending too much time alone.

It can sometimes be a dangerous thing to be alone with only one's thoughts to entertain.

Wren misses her husband. Her greatest wish at this moment is that he be sitting right beside her, telling a corny joke and giving her one of his comforting hugs.

# INHALE, EXPEL, TO HELL

Wren spends the rest of the day staying busy. She washes the floors, even washes the walls and organizes the junk drawer, getting rid of whatever isn't useful anymore: old batteries, small light bulbs, elastic bands. She tosses them out and says a prayer to her kohkum and other angels that surround asking to guide her and keep her safe from harm. She prays to Creator that she isn't losing her mind and that she's able to find calm and peace. She gives thanks, too, and asks that her day be filled with joy.

Wren finishes the kids' pinch pots, readying them for delivery back to tiny hands. She's expecting her husband to return home later this afternoon, so she's already thawed a beef brisket that'll go in the smoker outdoors. Its flavours will have succulently blended by the time Lord returns to the farmhouse. The neighbour boys arrive, as they always do any time there's work that needs to be done. They remove the snow from the parking area and out to the long road leading to the main highway. It brings a smile to Wren's face as she looks out the kitchen window to see a nice, cleared driveway.

Her feeling of warmth is short lived, however, as she notices there is still a big pile of snow blocking Raven's car still parked in the yard. Wren thinks that keeping her sister's vehicle is a signal of hope that someday Raven will return. She imagines every single day that Raven will come back and keeps the image of her sister's smiling face close to her heart. Wren decides to smudge before leaving the house. Too much time alone in an empty house brings out ghosts.

She will deliver the kids' pinch pots before heading out to do errands. She places some dried sage in a pottery bowl she constructed in her sister's honour. Again, she asks for strength: "Please God, help me to carry my thoughts through this day in a good way. And my heart is still hurting. Help me to see goodness so that I may do good in this world."

Wren's usual routine is to head to town, grab a gas station coffee and say hello to whichever neighbours happen to be out and about at that time. Today, though, she'll vary this. Wren can't help but remember the dream she had when she laid down for a short nap. That ominous scarecrow sitting beside her in the living room. *Is it true what it said about Father Hector? Is it real or just another nightmare?* To Wren, it seemed as real as a regular conversation. The detailed descriptions, the foreshadowing of bad intent...

Wren wonders if she's supposed to stop him. Now that she's killed once, can she again? The little restaurant Scarecrow described is an actual place located on the outskirts of the city. Wren decides she can go there today to pick up her coffee. She wants to see if Renée exists to greet her as Wren enters the establishment. She wants to see if there really is a table of locals and regulars who meet every day to discuss the woes of the world and thoughts for the day. She wants to see if the priest is a part of that gathering crowd. There was a photo of him in the newspaper and an even more vivid picture of his face in her thoughts while she slept. She's sure she'll recognize him if he's there.

# LIAR, LIAR, PANTS ON FIRE

It is surreal for Wren to pull open the heavy door to the coffee shop where the retired priest regularly holds court over a cup of coffee and a half-priced, day-old muffin. Before entering, she fumbles to put her car keys in her jacket pocket and drops them on the sidewalk. It's then that a kindly voice offers to help. "Here, let me get that for you."

Wren finds herself face to face with the very man she's travelled here to find. Uncanny, but maybe not a coincidence. As he offers to open the door to the restaurant for her, Wren excuses herself, explaining that she's left something behind in her car. She is unnerved when Father Hector reaches out and holds her elbow. She doesn't want him to touch her.

Wren doesn't go in because she doesn't want to know if Renée is there to greet her wearing a warm smile and a white cardigan. She decides it'll be too much to gaze into that innocent face, knowing what Scarecrow told her. Wren wonders if the girl will be fondled by this old bastard and lets out a few tears and gasps for air. The very thought has taken her breath away.

The encounter with Father Hector has shaken her and she finds herself driving to the gas station located in the same strip mall as the restaurant. She needs a cup of coffee, so she heads in to the gas station to purchase one along with a pack of cigarettes, even though she doesn't smoke. Because she doesn't have a lighter in her purse, she asks the cashier for a pack of matches.

Traffic is still heavy, just at the tail end of the lunch rush, so Wren decides to sit in her vehicle in the parking lot for a while until it passes. After lighting up a cigarette, she immediately feels light-headed, a feeling that extends to her stomach, making her queasy. She thinks of the moment that old priest reached out to touch her, and once again her mind drifts to thoughts of her sister.

It may have been the nicotine pulsing through her system that causes Wren to turn to thoughts of revenge toward the man responsible for leaving such deep hurts in her family—or it could have been her glance at her rear-view mirror showing retired pastor carrying a paper cup and walking happily to his vehicle.

Wren watches Father Hector get into his car and drive away. Without thinking, she follows him.

# THOU SHALT NOT COVET

Wren stalks Father Hector for the next four days, making sure to keep her distance. She heads to the city immediately after Lord leaves home each morning. Mostly, she uses her days to fine-tune her plan. *Has this man committed such atrocities that he deserves a reckoning?* As much as Wren examines any feelings of guilt at the question, the answer always comes out in the affirmative. Next, she considers how she can approach him and how she can gain his trust enough to lure him to her home in the country.

Wren knows she must be strategic and plan Father Hector's demise for a time when Lord is away again. Lord has told her he needs to make a trip to Manitoba tomorrow and will be gone for three or four days. This time he suggested that she come with him, but Wren declined the offer saying she has a new commission she needs to work on. She doesn't tell him that her new project means burning bones.

Wren decides she will tell Father Hector that she's going to have a baby. He knows nothing about her other than she is a young lady asking for help and spiritual guidance. She will ask him to come out and bless her house, particularly the baby's room.

She tells herself that her true plans are a blessing to the world, to put an end to Father Hector's tyranny. The courts didn't stop him, the police didn't gather convincing evidence and they chose not to accept testimony from women still living with the horrific memory of sexual abuse. It all happened too long ago, authorities said. There is no proof, no witnesses, they said. As if Father Hector's freedom from the law weren't bad enough, there was further victimization to those who brought the charges, with lawyers even going so far as to suggest that the advanced ages of the "alleged victims" meant their memories might be flawed.

Wren is disgusted by the very sight of the old priest. She's been watching his routine and has learned that he is a creature of habit, driving the short distance from the seniors' home where he lives to the coffee shop every morning except Sunday. He gets into his car at 9:50 a.m. and is seated, having ordered a coffee and muffin, by ten. He chooses from the day-old muffins, always putting in his first request for a banana-pecan muffin. If they don't have banana-pecan, his second choice is always chocolate chip. His coffee order is one milk, one sugar. He drinks two cups because the refill is free.

Today, Wren is within earshot. She has hurriedly ordered a coffee to go and is finally able to meet young Renée. Wren is sad to see a fake pearl necklace around her small neck.

The courts declared there was no proof that Father Hector caused harm while he worked at the residential school, but Wren knows that her kohkum would never lie. Wren never did question her grandmother for details, it was too painful to do so, but she knows Father Hector is the one who crushed Auntie Dodi's spirit and why her life fell apart. Father Hector killed a part of Dodi's soul as he groped her and molested her. She was just a young girl. He left torturing memories lasting a lifetime, a descent into a hell Dodi couldn't escape from, no matter how hard she tried with vodka and sleeping pills.

The courts let Father Hector walk free but Wren will not. And does she feel guilty? No. That's not the right word. Does she feel vengeance? That's not the right feeling. What goes through her mind in the moments before Wren approaches Father Hector is this: she wants to take the pain and anguish that he caused and turn it into something to help others.

Like the first time she followed him, watching through her rearview mirror from the parking lot, Wren waits for him again. She's seen historical photos of how Indigenous children were forced to dress in residential schools: hair cut short, the girls in plain cotton dresses and leather shoes. It's how Wren is dressed today, having visited the local

Salvation Army thrift store. She's pulled her long hair back from her face and up into a ponytail. The historical photos show no display of jewellery or adornment, but Wren decides to wear her kohkum's pink, plastic rosary. Sometimes a wound needs to be reopened in order to heal.

The moment Wren has been waiting for presents itself. Wren sees Father Hector leave the coffee shop carrying a brown to-go bag. Likely another day-old muffin. Wren closes her eyes and sees Kohkum as a girl. Sees her Auntie Dodi as a girl. She takes a deep breath, opens the car door and steps out.

"Father Hector," Wren says. She smiles and holds out her hand in greeting. "My name is Sarah." She feels no guilt offering a false name. Names are sacred and he doesn't need to know Wren's. *All this old perv cares about is the possibility of getting laid,* she thinks to herself, *and I will lay something on him, that's for sure.* As these wicked thoughts pass through Wren's mind, only a smile remains on her face—urging, ever urging Father Hector closer to the flame.

Wren invites the retired pastor to her home. "I hope you don't mind me asking a favour, but I wanted the blessing of someone like you. I found your name in a registry. Hector. That was the name of my own father," she lies. "He is no longer with us, bless his soul, but I know he is watching from heaven and blessing the baby's room would be important to him, as it is to me. I hoped you would do this for me and my husband. If you are not too busy now, of course," she says. "I can drive you out to our home and bring you back to the city after. I would be so grateful to know that my baby's room will have a proper blessing. Please say yes."

Father Hector agrees, all the while staring at Wren's breasts. He comments on the pink rosary she's wearing. He tells her it's lovely.

# INTO THE CONFESSIONAL

"My husband should be home soon," says Wren as they leave the parking lot. Wren is starting to feel much more comfortable being dishonest. "The plan is to have the baby's room painted by this afternoon."

"And do you and your husband know whether you are expecting a girl or a boy?" Father Hector inquires.

"No," Wren replies. "We decided to wait until our baby is born. Whether a girl or boy, we are blessed. Thank you so much for helping us out on such short notice. Neither my husband nor I go to church on a regular basis, but prayer has always been important to my family, especially to my grandmother."

"Is your grandmother still with us?" Father Hector asks.

"No, Father. Sadly, she passed several years ago. She is precious in my memory. The baby's room is sure to be extra special. It's where my grandma used to keep all her craft supplies when I was a little girl. We spent a lot of time in that room making jewellery or sewing."

A conversation of small talk doesn't prepare Wren for Father Hector's next request, as she signals toward the freeway.

"Well, I am happy to bestow a blessing," he says, "and thanks for driving. I'd probably get lost driving in the country. Besides, now that I am up in years, my licence has been restricted. I'm not allowed to drive on the highway anymore," he shares. "It's good to be asked to keep prayer and faith. Now that I'm retired, I have the time in my day for a special request like this. I wonder," he says slowly, "if we might stop by my place before we leave the city?"

As the priest takes a sip of coffee from his paper mug, Wren searches for a plausible reason to keep driving out of town and not go anywhere where the two might be seen together. She knows if she stops at the seniors' home where Father Hector lives, some nosy neighbour will be gawking out the window, a neighbour who may remember her later during questioning.

"I'd like to pick up my prayer book and my rosary," Father Hector explains.

Wren fidgets ever so slightly and nervously runs her fingers over the pink rosary that hangs from her neck. She tells him she's hoping he can use Kohkum's old rosary because it has such meaning to her and has been in the family for decades. She mentions that she has a Bible at her home and that she and her husband have already picked out certain passages that hold special significance to them both.

"Oh, good to hear. Which ones?"

It isn't amazing that Wren is able to cite Proverb 3:9–10. "Honour the Lord with your wealth, with the fruits of all your crops; then your barns will be filled to overflowing, and your vats will brim over with new wine," she says.

This particular proverb is one Wren read while waiting in line at the gas station the other day. As is so often the case, customers don't come into the gas station just to purchase something, they also come to visit, which means polite conversation about grandkids, what's on the stove for supper tonight and, of course, the weather. It can mean that a quick trip can turn into having to wait around awhile. While she was waiting the other day, Wren picked up one of those community news bulletins which lets everyone know important things like recycling days and so on. Proverb 3:9-10 was printed on the back of the bulletin. Wren liked the message, so she committed it to memory.

She likes to remember phrases and sayings, believing it keeps the mind sharp. For that reason, she's always enjoyed a good game of Scrabble and other word games that help to expand the vocabulary. Like the word *sluggard*. It brings Wren a momentary bit of joy as she remembers the last time she and Raven played the game. There was almost a fist fight because Raven thought Wren made up the word *sluggard* until Wren pulled out the dictionary. "See, there it is!" she yelled, hardly able to stop laughing. "It means 'habitually lazy person.'" Eleven points!"

"That proverb is one my grandmother used to read to me," explains Wren.

Wren is convincing and the explanation seems to soften the heart of the old priest, who finally agrees that it is proper to use Kohkum's old rosary and Bible. There will be no need to make a trip to the seniors' home after all.

Any anxiety Wren feels at her own impending plan is quickly erased as she glances at her passenger. She notices he's rubbing his hands together while he looks out the window. It sickens Wren to know what those hands have done. What they still do. She can't help but think it's like watching a fly rub its filthy legs together.

# TURNING POINT

Wren tries to ensure the conversation with Father Hector stays amicable during the half-hour drive back to the farmhouse. She talks about the baby and how she's looking forward to teaching the child how to skate, how to ride a bike, how to swim and how to collect frogs in the stream that runs through the property. As they turn down Wren's long driveway, Wren announces that she doesn't see her husband's truck as expected. Another lie. She feels like she is shaking but hopes she displays no visible signs of discomfort. She invites the padre into her home. The smell of cinnamon and apples still lingers in her kitchen.

The morning sun catches the sparkle of brown sugar granules that garnish the apple crisp she baked earlier this morning. The dessert was set out to cool on the counter. She offers a piece to her guest.

"I have some thick cream as well. That's how I always eat my crisp," she says. Her visitor accepts the offer and Wren begins to spoon some of the sweet dish onto a plate.

Father Hector has no way of knowing the dessert has been laced with sleeping pills. Wren ground up four in her mortar and pestle, adding the powder before popping the crisp into the oven. The ingredient was strategically placed in the left-hand corner of the pan. She serves him a generous portion from that corner. As the priest gobbles up the sweetness, he can't help but comment on Wren's collection of pottery displayed around the kitchen.

"I love working with clay because it comes from the earth," Wren explains. "There is something that's comforting to me about knowing we share our meals using a plate that's been created from a part of nature."

"Interesting-looking piece of pottery," Father Hector remarks, referring to the vase with the bone black finish. Wren looks at it and pictures Billy Vespas burning in the kiln. "It reminds me of an artifact from those historical recreations of the Bible seen in film," continues Father Hector.

"Ancient Egyptian pottery," Wren agrees. "It's something I've been experimenting with. Telling stories of hunting and gathering. Death and destruction using petroglyph images. There are clues to the past in each of the crude drawings." Catching herself becoming distracted by the priest's conversation, Wren pulls back. "I'm glad you like the pottery design," she says, thinking of how he, too, will soon be burned and turned into a similar piece. By the time Wren finishes her sentence, old Father Hector has fallen off his stool. His head hits the hardwood floor with a thud and his nose begins to bleed.

"I'll tell your story, too, you sick fuck. Never again will your filthy hands bring harm. You murderer. You killed my auntie's spirit. You made my kohkum's heart sad. You raped those girls," Wren says to the unconscious man on the floor.

Wren bends over the man's limp body and checks his pulse. It's slow, but still there. For now. She checks her image in a nearby mirror, a tile experiment Wren undertook when Lord brought home some leftover materials of broken tile and glass. Maybe it is a lack of sleep or a guilty conscience, but for a split second, Wren feels a sense of terror. Is her mind playing tricks on her? Wren is certain that in the reflection of that mirror, she has seen the face of Lord's mother, a woman she has never met, only seen in photos. Most notably, the photo of her corpse laying in the coffin. The photo she's hidden in the upstairs guest bedroom. Suddenly, Wren thinks she hears a whisper. More like a rasp. It's that same voice she remembers hearing from Scarecrow in her dream the other day.

"It's got a disease. Kill it, burn it, remove it."

The image reflecting in the mirror is visible for less than a few seconds, the time it takes for a shooting star to be seen. Wren goes to the sink to pour herself a glass of cold water, splashing some of the liquid on her face.

"What am I doing?" she asks aloud.

"Bury that dust speck. Make it disappear," the raspy voice replies.

As if in a trance, Wren makes her way up the large staircase to the upstairs bathroom. She retrieves another vial of Lord's insulin. He's just had his prescription renewed so probably won't miss it. She goes to the spare room where she keeps her craft supplies. The same room her grandmother used for the same purpose of making beautiful things with her hands.

She digs around in the basket of ribbons and pulls out a clean syringe. Almost floating, Wren returns to the kitchen, the loaded needle in her hand. She feels no remorse as she injects the heart-stopping serum into the old priest's abdomen. "A missing person you will become," she proclaims, standing over the body. "You will sin no more. Ashes to ashes, asshole. Do you think the RCMP will ignore your disappearance, too, like my sister's? Do you think anyone will notice you are gone?"

Wren injects Father Hector in the belly three times, knowing that soon he will be no more. He will harm no more. It is time to stoke the fire in her outdoor kiln again.

Before exiting her kitchen, Wren removes one of Father Hector's winter boots. Size eight with a leather design. She figures she'll paint it indigo and prop it up on her fence post. Even though she's never thought of herself as a collector of trophies, it seems she has become one. Father Hector's boot will hang in plain view where everyone can see but no one will ask twice about.

# THERE ARE NO QUIET MOMENTS

Lord is gone for another few days. Some type of "rejuvenation of a historic building" in Winnipeg this time. Good. No one other than God needs to witness Wren straining her back as she drags the dead body of the priest toward her outdoor kiln. His dragging feet leave a trail in the snow, which no one will see other than that coyote who watches from a distance. He's showed up again and Wren wonders what stories he tells when he returns to his pack each night. Is he looking for food?

For a second, Wren ponders that she might undress the body and leave it in the gully instead of firing it in her kiln. The coyote pack will take care of disposal she's sure. She decides it's too risky Instead, she elects to mutilate the body as Father Hector so insidiously ravaged those of countless children. Wren takes an axe into her hands. She swings at the priest's elbows, then in two bone-crunching swipes, Wren severs his hands.

Wren abandons the corpse, carrying the butchered parts toward the area the coyote has been pacing. She's careful not to allow any drops of blood on her parka. Blood splatters cover the snow, but she'll pile more snow on the stains later. Ultimately it will absorb into the ground. She thinks of the pink rosary still hanging around her neck and asks for her kohkum's forgiveness. An eye for an eye? A profane diatribe comes from Wren's lips as she hurls each limb toward the snow-covered coulee at the edge of her property. The rest of his body will meet the flames in a few hours. That's how long it will take for rigor mortis to set in, making it easier for Wren to push a stiffened corpse into the mouth of the kiln.

Wren adds more wood to the kiln. She will fire it up once the body is inside. It has been the better part of a day so far—stalking, lying, luring and lacing the old man's blood. She decides to take a break and enjoy a bonfire in her firepit located at the east side of her property. The house blocks any view of traffic travelling along the highway. All that can be seen from that vantage point is an idyllic view of an old farmhouse surrounded by cascades of fresh snow.

Wren decides she wants to dance. As the bonfire sparks to life, she opens the large door that leads to her studio. She turns up the volume on the stereo and selects the Andino Suns' "Weichafe" again. Wren sets the song to repeat. She turns it up loud so the music can be heard outdoors by the fire, where she will dance freely. A ceremony. Wren grabs a bundle of sage she picked earlier in the summer. Now dry, she'll offer it to the fire: to spirit, to say prayers and swear her benevolence that what she's done was the right thing to do. Wren will pray for Father Hector's soul, that he returns to his maker and is made to repent.

With the sound of music piercing the cold air, Wren moves to the rhythm, dancing around the fire as the stiffening corpse lays in wait. The coyote comes to take the hands and limbs offered to him. Wren watches as he disappears behind the bush that extends to the edge of the lake. As Wren moves, offering sage to the fire, she enters a trance-like state. She can see images spark from the flames. Scarecrow. She sees the smiling face of Raven on the last day they saw each other. Her kohkum, sitting quietly in her farmhouse kitchen and knitting a pair of warm socks. The coyote. Wren sees light as she waves her hands toward the sky. Tears are streaming down her face. The crackle of fire, the sound of revolution in the music and the crunch of snow under her feet brings Wren long-awaited peace.

"You will harm no more!" she repeats, shouting at a cloudless sky. Wren drops to the ground and instinctively begins to flap her arms and move her legs in a large sweeping motion. For some reason, she feels compelled to make a snow angel. To mark the spot. To mark the day. "You will harm no more."

Wren passes out in the snow. The bonfire is nothing but red coals when she awakes. Her muscles ache as she feeds pieces of wood to her kiln. She'll hoist in what remains of the old man once she regains her strength. Wren decides to go back in to the farmhouse, wiping the snow from her leggings as she walks through the open door. It occurs to her that she's hungry, that she hasn't eaten all day.

She checks the refrigerator and sees the makings for a sandwich, but instead of reaching for the ham, lettuce and mustard, her hand goes toward a basket of strawberries. She remembers her kohkum telling her that eating strawberries cures heartache. The shape of the sweet fruit resembles the shape of a human heart and the many seeds on the berry are a reminder that planting good seeds will grow love, hope and magic. Something Wren desperately needs. Love. Hope. Magic.

And forgiveness.

# HEALING THE HEART

*Murder is exhausting,* Wren thinks to herself as she pulls on a long fleece nightgown. It is red with white snowflakes and very warm. She decides to turn in for the night, even though it is much earlier than her usual bedtime. The smell of death still lingers outdoors. She's already pushed the old priest's body into the kiln and fired up the wood. The smell of burning hair and bones turns her stomach. To help force the smell away, she dabs a drop of lavender oil under her nose. She's always been told that its sweet scent will help her sleep.

Wren closes her eyes but restful slumber is not where she goes. It is a nightmare again. The coyote is there. She hears the searing of flesh from inside the kiln—like Spam in a frying pan, sizzling and spitting under intense heat. She hears the coyote crunching the bones of one of the priest's hands. There is blood, which doesn't gush but instead oozes from torn flesh like molasses.

The coyote yelps as the priest's other hand reaches up and grabs the animal by the ear. The flesh on that rogue hand has already started to rot but it pulls hard on the coyote's ear until the canine runs into the bush. Then it grips the snow with bony fingers, pulling itself closer and closer toward the farmhouse. Scarecrow is watching and lets out a sinister cackle. They are coming for her. For Wren.

Wren's nightmare changes. Now she sees Kohkum standing in front of her doorway. Kohkum holds the pink rosary in one hand and a braid of sweetgrass in the other. Raven is standing next to her. Kohkum says a few words in Cree. *Mahti sipwehte kisewatisiwin ochi.* Leave now with kindness. It is spoken with both the reverence of a prayer and the authority of a command. Scarecrow disappears, turning to ash and disappearing into the fresh snow. The hand continues to advance until Raven picks up the axe leaning against the house and brings it down with one hard blow, almost severing it in two.

The coyote runs from the darkness of the bush and grabs the hand. It flops on the ground like a fish out of water until it's crushed in the strong jaws of the hungry animal. Kohkum makes the sign of the cross and both she and Raven disappear into the night. Like the tail of a shooting star, a light ascends toward the heavens, making Wren feel safe. Nothing bad shall be allowed to cross over her threshold.

Whatever has been done needed to be done. As Wren awakens from sleep, she too makes the sign of the cross, lifts her arms toward the sky and bids her grandmother good night. "Kisakihitin Kohkum. I love you Grandmother and thank you. Raven, I miss you. Kinanaskomitin."

It is important to Wren to speak in the old language, the language those in the spirit world will understand. She wipes a tear from her eye and in the dark, says another prayer for forgiveness.

# NO NEWS IS GOOD NEWS

Wren has done her best to make sure no clues are left behind, other than boots on the fence post and stories in petroglyph images on her bone black pottery. Ashes of the dead. It's been three days since she put that old man in her kiln. He's ash now. Burned him up so that God won't even recognize him.

She knows Father Hector left his car in the parking lot of the strip mall where she'd been stalking him. She figures that eventually the car will get towed away and put into the police impound where someone can purchase it at auction at some later date. *But surely, she thinks, someone is bound to notice he hasn't returned to the seniors' home, or that he no longer goes to the coffee shop to order a day-old muffin?*

Wren sees nothing in the newspaper, which she peruses while standing at the gas station. She's going to head to the city again with a grocery list. As she turns on her ignition, news radio comes to life. She wants to know if there's a story about Father Hector, but there is nothing on the news about a missing priest. This surprises her, considering the coverage of his recent acquittal.

Wren wonders if no one cares about him, thinks that maybe others secretly wondered if all the testimonies were true. Wren supposes that someday soon, people will notice he's missing. But then, people go missing all the time. Wren pauses for a second, realizing the irony of her own thoughts.

None of the news really interests Wren. The newscaster talks about a decline in home sales, a union somewhere planning a strike. She is just about to change the station when a story comes on that makes her blood boil.

"A verdict has been reached in the case of Myron Salt." the news anchor announces. "Minutes ago, the judge presiding over the case found him not guilty in the death of Mavis Blind, the fifteen-year-old girl found deceased in a farmer's field near Southey over a year ago. We have a reporter at the courthouse."

Wren listens to the familiar details about the girl's disappearance. The reporter goes on to say that the young lady left a house party around midnight in the city's North Central area last year. Young Mavis didn't have enough money to cover the cost of a cab ride to her home on the George Gordon First Nation near Punnichy, deciding to hitchhike instead.

It wasn't until the following spring that a farmer discovered her body while he was out seeding. Her half-naked corpse was found stuffed under a round hay bale. The not-guilty verdict was reached because there was no forensic evidence and there were no eyewitnesses. The reporter ended the update by explaining that the twenty-one-year-old accused of the crime was pronounced free and led out a back door of the courthouse as the Blind family was left in the courtroom, visibly shaken.

It's too much for Wren. Too many real-life stories about evil men causing destruction and seemingly never taking responsibility for their actions. Wren feels like she hears stories like this every week and all she ever hears anyone say is that it's tragic these things happen. They never offer a solution, always figuring the answer lies somewhere else.

"Not this time, Myron Salt," Wren mutters while wiping away a tear.

Wren finds herself stopped at the shoulder of the highway, radio still blaring. She can't remember why she is pulled over or what she is looking for, and in these moments, Wren is not herself. She enters a fugue state again—a place where her actions have a life of their own, without memory, without accountability. When she checks the clock on the dashboard, she sees that a whole hour has passed.

She wants to scream because of the last thing she heard on the news. Another young girl is dead and the person accused of killing her is free. Wren begins to beat the dashboard, yelling as she does. Raven is gone and there was no investigation. Billy Vespas was violent and a rapist—no one brought him to justice. That old perverted priest was pronounced innocent of his crimes, even though Wren knows he deserved much worse. Now this. No more.

"Justice will be served," Wren promises to an empty car. "And your dark filth will be wiped clean with the fresh snowfall."

Her thoughts go back to the day Mavis's body was discovered. She cries as she listens to the news story, it makes her think about Raven again. *What if this was a story about her?* Wren screams in anger as she slams her fist on the dashboard again. She knows she'll have to regain her composure soon. She straightens her shirt and pulls her hair away from her face. *It's a good day*, like she told herself upon waking, despite the tragic news on the radio. *It's a good day because Lord is coming home this afternoon.* He's been gone over a week and as much as she's grateful that he hasn't been home these past days, she also misses him. She's looking forward to preparing him one of his favourite meals: a slow-cooked beef stew.

Wren restarts the car and turns back onto the highway. As she reaches the outskirts of the city, she decides to practise breathing techniques learned in yoga class. "Inhale goodness, peace and love," she tells herself. "Exhale sadness, worry and despair." It helps to calm her and allows her to let feelings of fury and rage subside. Any plans that she might think of for Myron will come to her later, when she's alone with her thoughts. She will figure out where Myron Salt lives, where he works, where he hangs out. For now, she has a grocery list that needs her attention and a lovely evening with her husband awaits.

After she visits the grocery store, Wren checks the time. Lord's flight lands in half an hour and she wants to make sure she gets to the airport before his plane does. The traffic flow is light at this time of day, which means Wren has plenty of time to find a parking stall. Her early arrival at the terminal means she has some time to look around the airport gift shop, too. There are so many corny souvenirs, like a fish replica covered in bits of fur and a sign that boasts: *Saskatchewan lake fish.*

The shop also carries beautiful, handmade jewellery made by local artists, but all the pieces are for women. There are also fresh flowers. Wren buys Lord a red rose. a symbol of their love and an affirmation to herself that she will do her best to focus on the joy in her life, putting an end to dark thoughts and deeds. He has gone out of his way to be patient these past months but she fears his patience might be running out. She misses the days when they used to tell each other that they loved one another. She misses knowing what he ate for lunch. She misses the trust that she'd see each time he looked into her eyes. She misses his touch.

Now, she has no idea what he might see when he gazes into her face. As Wren absent-mindedly runs her finger down the rose's stem, she pricks her finger on a thorn. She tunes out as a bright red droplet of blood slowly makes its way from the wound, carrying her thoughts back to the dark place.

# IF I EVER

Wren's husband is arriving within minutes and she feels as though she doesn't have the time to plot and ponder, but she is seeing images again. She can't figure out if they are hallucinations due to lack of sleep, or premonitions from the Ancestors. *Am I going crazy?* she wonders. *Or am I opening up? And if I am, what am I opening up to?*

Wren can hear that raspy phantom voice calling out again as she feels a trickle of blood make its way toward her wrist, staining the white blouse she's wearing. She travels again to a place unknown and unfriendly. A dream? A hallucination? Whatever the cause, Wren can no longer sit peacefully in the airport foyer as she was doing moments earlier.

The light in the airport changes and the air hangs like a fog. Wren sees the face of her beloved sister. She is screaming. Filthy hands are clawing at Raven's neck and grasping her windpipe until her eyes roll back. Her final breath is that of pain. Next, she sees an image of Mavis Blind. Wren has seen her face before on a missing person's bulletin early last winter. The face of the young girl is wild with fear, the same look that coyote gave when the severed hand of Father Hector tried to pull off its ear. There is nowhere for Mavis to run.

The scene changes. Now Wren is standing in the farmer's field, watching as Myron slashes the girl's neck with a hunting knife. It looks handcrafted with a thick blade and a bone handle. Wren screams for him to stop, but no sound comes from her mouth. Myron cannot hear her words and doesn't stop his attack. The girl's neck spurts in violent torment. The blood gushing from the cut makes a hideous sound, like the howling of a wicked wind, and rushes from her body in a torrent. There is no helping her now. Her heart stops. The white snow beside the hay bale turns red and the young girl's light is snuffed out for good.

As quickly as she left, Wren is back in the airport waiting area. A young man with a guitar strapped to his back has noticed Wren's erratic breathing. From a bystander's point of view, Wren looks to be in pain and he gently places his hand on her shoulder for comfort.

"Ma'am are you okay?" he asks gently.

"Oh, yes. Sorry, sorry. I must have dozed off for a second. Insomnia." Wren sits up straight and attempts to regain her composure.

"I know all about sleeplessness," he says and smiles. "Been on the road for weeks now with my wife. Both musicians." He stops and smiles at Wren again. There is concern on his face. "Her flight is coming in. Are you meeting someone special, too? I can't help but notice the rose."

"The most special," Wren replies. "My husband's been gone for the past week. Can't say I will ever get used to him having to travel so much for work, but I can say that every time I see him again, it's like the first time we met."

"Lucky man," he says before quickly turning his attention toward the escalator carrying passengers from Arrivals. "There's my girl." His enthusiasm weakens Wren's anger as she watches the young man rush toward his wife and into an embrace. Wren looks down at the rose in her hands. Lord's return home is comforting, signalling a return to cherishing present moments and turning her attention to what is good in her life.

She considers the idea of simply forgetting about the images she has just seen in her imagination. She can try, she thinks, to erase those horrifying thoughts of murder, and with them, the anger bubbling just beneath the surface, threatening to consume her.

# BREATHING NEW LIFE

Wren sees her husband descending on the escalator and greets him with a rose and a smile. Lord puts his hand on her cheek and gives her a short but affectionate kiss on the forehead. When they get out to the parking lot, Lord holds back Wren's long hair so it doesn't fly loose in her face as she opens the trunk for his carry-on.

After a moment, Lord looks at Wren with a deep and sensuous stare, announcing, "I have decided to take a 'stay-cation' next week. I've missed you so much these past days. We need to spend more time together." Then he kisses her, long and hard, before suggesting, "I can drive back home if you like. Maybe we'll stop off somewhere on the way and get an order to go."

"That's not necessary," she says. "I've already picked up the ingredients for one of your favourites, which I will be slow roasting at home soon. I've missed you, too, Lord. I am so happy you're back."

Wren touches Lord's hand on the steering wheel as he makes the turn north and toward busy Lewvan Drive in the direction back to the valley.

"If you want, though, we can stop off somewhere and pick up a nice bottle of wine for dinner," suggests Wren.

"I've already got one of your favourites packed away in my suit-case. Found it at a specialty shop a couple of days ago. Another great variety from the Okanagan."

"Sounds like a plan," Wren replies and turns on the radio.

She changes the station from news to FM Radio Two. It's classical hour and the music is soothing to match the couple's mood. They haven't made any plans yet for a trip to a sunny destination, but Wren is happy that Lord will be staying home for the next several days.

Once back at the farmhouse and through the front door, Lord is greeted by a delicious aroma: Wren has made an apple and berry crisp. Wren comes in seconds after and starts unloading the groceries she bought for a nice, hearty stew. She starts to set the butcher block island which they use as a table. She stops, however, when Lord suggests he build a fire in the stone fireplace in the living room.

"We can set up on the coffee table and spend the evening doing something a little more special," suggests Lord from the other room.

She likes the change in plans and takes her pottery plates out of the kitchen and into the living room as Lord unzips his carry-on to retrieve the bottle of Ehrenfelser, a peach, pear and anise wine, one of Wren's favourites.

It's a peaceful and romantic scene, allowing Wren to momentarily forget what went on in their home while Lord was away. She had worried that some residual negative energy might stick to the walls and ceilings, the way spiderwebs do, but nothing of the kind lingers. As the fire crackles, there is tender conversation.

After the meal, Lord turns on some music and invites Wren to dance, "Right here in the living room," he says. "We can spend the whole night by this fire." He holds his wife close in a slow waltz, inviting Wren to melt into his embrace. He slowly unzips the zipper along the back of Wren's dress. She lets it fall to the floor.

# HAPPY WIFE, HAPPY LIFE

The couple never did make it up to their second-floor bedroom that night in front of the fire. They slept on the living room floor, directly in front of the mantel, holding each other and covered by the warm, knitted afghan that is usually draped at the edge of the couch.

The sun is already up when Wren is awakened by the sound of the coffee machine brewing in the kitchen and the sounds of Lord chopping wood outside. As she watches him through the kitchen window, she can't help but think of the ways the axe has been used while Lord was away, ways only she will ever know. She makes a conscious decision not to ruin a perfectly beautiful start to this calm, sunny day and she banishes the thoughts of severed limbs from her head just as quickly as they arrived.

Coffee is ready and Wren detects a hint of chicory among the freshly ground beans. It makes her smile to know that Lord likely picked up this special roast at the same specialty store where he found last night's wine. As she pours herself a mug of the hot brew, Wren figures that if her husband is chopping wood outdoors, it will be a bit of time before he comes back in, so she decides to surprise him by making a nice breakfast.

As she sips, she reaches for a cookbook on a shelf that Lord constructed between two windows. Wren glances back towards the living room; it fills her with a deep sense of joy to have spent such time with her husband, joy Wren hasn't felt for a long time because such worry and turmoil has surrounded them these last months.

Things Wren couldn't tolerate. Lies, harm and mayhem all aimed at women just like her, brown women. It's a poison that spreads and grows like alkali choking out the land. Now, however, Wren feels a sense of satisfaction knowing that she's done what she can to stop it, secrets between her and God.

Wren smiles again as she looks at the afghan, now just a lump on the floor in front of the fireplace. Wren makes a mental note that she'll tidy up in that room later. For now though, she's decided that a quiche will be what greets her husband when he comes back in from chopping logs. The rose that Wren brought for Lord at the airport is already displayed in a vase and sunlight streams in through the kitchen window.

As the sweet aroma of caramelizing onions fills her kitchen, Wren runs her fingers across the amethyst pendant Lord attached around her neck last night before handing her a glass of wine. She's always loved the purple stone, even more after reading that its healing properties include purifying the mind and clearing away negative thinking. That's not the reason Lord purchased the gift, though. He'd just seen it in a shop window in downtown Winnipeg and thought it would look nice on his wife. He is also well aware that Wren loves gifts that come from Mother Earth.

One reason Lord decided to take a few days off this coming week is because he wants to help Wren get ready for a new show where her work will be featured. It's a special time for any artist to have their own solo exhibit. He said he could see that the outdoor kiln was fired while he was away and says he's proud of her for working again. Splitting logs this morning is his way of saying that he'll be there for her, to help feed the fire and get her new pieces ready for the show.

"Wow, smells great in here," Lord exclaims as he comes through the door.

Wren is popping the shrimp, cheese, asparagus and onion dish into the oven. Before taking off his boots, he grabs her from behind to give her a satisfying hug.

"But what smells even better, is the scent of you. You were wonderful last night," he whispers into her hair.

Wren closes the oven door then turns to share in his embrace. "Oh, my love, you are all sweaty," she says and giggles. "We have forty minutes before this properly bakes. Maybe you want to take a shower first," she suggests, caressing his jaw.

"Maybe you want to come with me," he says.

"Oh yes, you insatiable, handsome man. That can be done."

Lord takes Wren by the hand and leads her up the stairs toward the master bathroom.

"You're still wearing your coat. Here, let me get that," Wren says as she seductively unzips his navy jacket.

"And you are still wearing your apron." Lord runs his hand along the ponytail his wife always wears while cooking. "Let me get that." Lord turns on the shower and the couple step in. They are naked, vulnerable, in love.

*This is how it should be,* Wren thinks. *Trust and tenderness.* She squeezes a dab of lavender-scented body wash in her palm, then caresses her husband. While sweat is rinsed away, their passion provides more heat than the cascading droplets of water. "You are so beautiful, Wren," Lord whispers.

By the time they return to the kitchen, forty minutes has long passed, and the quiche is a little overcooked, but neither of them notice. They sit contentedly at the kitchen island where they have a view of sunlight gleaming off the fresh snow outside. A perfect start to a new day.

# UNVEILING NEW WORKS

These past days have been good for Wren, allowing her to focus on her marriage, to focus on her art. Lord has been her constant and affectionate companion since he returned from his latest business trip. His idea for a stay-cation was a good one. They've spent more time in bed than even in their early days of courtship. He's been with her in the studio each afternoon, even venturing into creating his own works, and feeding the fire for the outdoor kiln. They've been firing dozens of pieces, preparing for what will be an exciting show and pottery sale.

"I am digging this new style," Lord says, studying a vase. He doesn't know the piece has been finished with bone black ash, the very ash that used to be the skinny roofer. "This is different for you," he continues, picking up another. "The designs you've painted remind me of the ancient Egyptian pottery that was used to adorn the facades of tower entryways."

Lord is especially interested in a gargoyle image that Wren's thrown together using the ash of Father Hector. "Kind of maudlin but I like it," Lord says, running his fingers over the face of the wretched beast. "And, it's interesting because this type of work is exactly what the market is demanding again."

He talks about early architecture and how artists were as much a part of creation as the builders themselves. Wren already knows something about it because there was a similar discussion in one of her university classes. She doesn't stop him, however, finding comfort in listening to the sound of his voice, no matter what the subject.

Wren ponders the history of what she knows about gargoyles. The Catholic Church believed the grotesque figures would ward off evil.

The figures were often placed above doorways and gateways offering parishioners a sense of safety and protection within the sanctity of the church. *But what safety did that church bring to those touched by the hand of Father Hector?* Wren wonders, drawing the conclusion that a sense of safety comes from within the soul and not from within a building.

"Yes, I thought I would try something different," Wren replies once Lord is finished with his history lesson. "But I think of this as more of a garden ornament to scare those aphids away from eating my lettuce," she says and giggles.

Wren tells her husband that Kohkum used to place old, glass powerline insulators around her garden, explaining that the glass carried a memory and had the power to remind bugs to stay away. Her garden was always abundant, though she never figured out how to deal with the potato bugs underground.

It brings a warm smile to Wren's face to think of the moment Kohkum started swearing in Cree one autumn when the potato harvest was ready to dig up. *Wastakac* is a word that means "damn it," something Kohkum had never said before. It was the only profane word Wren ever remembers hearing in Cree. It's a phrase that she'd repeat, as a girl, anytime anything bothered her. Like when a schoolyard bully would make fun of her brown skin. *Wastakac!*

"My mom used to put out a scarecrow in the garden," Lord says. "She called it the Face of Doom and said that it would keep intruders away."

Wren gasps and holds her breath for a moment in disbelief. She excuses the sound as a hiccup, not wanting her husband to know he's upset her. Of course Lord would have no idea she has been having constant dreams about a scarecrow. His comment is surreal: does he somehow know her thoughts and fears?

While Lord continues to inspect and admire her new pottery pieces, Wren leaves for the farmhouse to retrieve their espresso machine. "I'll bring it out here so we can both enjoy a couple of cappuccinos."

"Sounds great," Lord agrees. "I'll continue packing up these pieces. You are going to have a spectacular show."

Wren feels guilt at the thought of keeping secrets from her husband, but decides to push all concerns out of her mind and commit to enjoying this day with Lord, free from harm, free from worry, free from sin. She whispers a prayer, barely audible, as she walks toward the front door.

# PUBLIC ADMISSION

Wren has never been much of a churchgoer, though she attends every once in a while on special occasions, so she feels no guilt about hosting the opening of her new exhibit on a Sunday. The past couple of weeks, she's been giving all her thoughts and efforts into her pottery.

What is occupying her now is unpacking the cardboard boxes filled with new work. Lord is helping her unload both her car and his own vehicle, carrying the heavy packages up a flight of stairs and into the spacious gallery. It's an excellent day for a show. There is no wind, no clouds in the sky, with the only sounds across the prairie being the many vehicles out and about. Wren hopes the drivers see the sandwich board she's placed out on the road, inviting everyone to come and visit this afternoon.

She says a silent prayer that her exhibit will be well-attended and gives thanks that lately, she seems to be more at peace now that her veil of sadness has been partially lifted. She offers her prayer upward and thinks about the acts she's recently undertaken. She has always figured that if a person is truly contrite or filled with sorrow about harmful acts they've committed, God already knows.

Wren doesn't feel the need to go to confession in these moments. To her, making an admission during confession seems more like talking to a counsellor or therapist. Wren isn't convinced that that type admission of guilt is necessary for her. She has rationalized that remorse, or even forgiveness, isn't needed given what those men did. She feels no remorse for ridding the world of hateful and damaged men, men who treated women like throw-away objects.

The stories of their demise are etched on some of the new pieces she's unveiling today. Those stories could so easily be deciphered by anyone knowing what to look for in the petroglyph designs decorating her bone black pottery. On an abstract mask, there is an image of a fish in the place of a mouth. Another piece, a heavy coffee mug, is decorated with a string of hand-painted pearls. It takes Wren, Lord and the gallery curator about three hours to set up all the pottery. Some pieces are hanging on the wall; others are displayed in cases. Wren has created dozens.

Just as they finish, there is the sound of footsteps outside. Next, the faint sound of a doorbell, signalling someone is entering the building. The curator greets the visitors, telling them to help themselves to some cookies, crackers and cheese that she's carefully set out in the lobby. "Here are some napkins, and there is coffee or tea in the corner if you like. Help yourself and enjoy while you look around." She gestures towards the main gallery area.

The guests are a mother and her daughter, out visiting in the valley for the day. They saw the sign out on the highway and decided to come in and have a look. "Oh Mom, you have to come take a look at this. I love it," exclaims the daughter. She tells Wren that her older sister is getting married in the spring. "We totally have to buy this for her, Mom."

"Oh, it's perfect," the mother replies. "And so different from other pottery we've been looking at." The girl and her mother admire the bone-black finish on their new wine decanter. Wren has painted images of the lake where that red truck belonging to the roofer is now permanently parked.

Lord stays the afternoon to help Wren with the opening, which is a good thing. Within the hour, he's the one looking after the cash box as Wren explains her new designs to the admiring public. (Well, a partial explanation—she'll never tell anyone where she got the bones for the bone black finish.)

"My love," Lord says during a quiet lull in crowd activity, "whatever you have been doing, you'll have to keep doing it. People love this work."

It's been such a great couple of weeks that Wren hasn't given any thought to Myron Salt and the story she heard on the news the day she picked up Lord at the airport. But now, as she watches visitors fussing over her new style of pottery, she promises Lord that she'll find a way to make more of the same. After all, she knows exactly where she'll get new material

# SCOUNDRELS

Lord's time at home was lovely, but business calls sooner than later. Lord must make another trip to Manitoba, driving out today. Wren will be alone with her thoughts again, thoughts of scorn and revenge towards those who cause harm but are never called to answer, who never face responsibility for what they've done. Maybe she would have tried stopping, but without realizing he'd done so, Lord has encouraged her. *Whatever you've been doing, keep doing it,* he'd said. Words that ring in her thoughts now.

Wren has tracked Myron's routine to a place called Scoundrels, a local watering hole that used to be frequented by many in Regina's north end before the freeway was constructed. It used to be a place where respectable people might pop in for a drink after work, but not anymore. Pasqua Street has become almost silent unless you listen for slurred and hushed whispers from the Scoundrels parking lot. Now, low-lifes hang out in dingy, sticky booths. Dank with despair, it's a place where dreams come to die, a place where all who visit seem to have abandoned their decency. Myron is one of them.

Wren parks her car in a parking lot with a falling-down fence tagged with graffiti and a garbage bin overflowing with debris. She sees a ragged scarecrow displayed in the front yard belonging to an area resident, across the street from the bar. That damn scarecrow. Wren hasn't seen it lately in her dreams, but now there is one staring at her. The face of doom.

As she sits in the car staring at the scarecrow, Wren wonders if the smallpox epidemic that used to exist throughout the land now exists within people's minds, eating away at everything sacred and good.

Wren decides then and there to see her actions tonight as eliminating the effects of this plague.

Wren has been following Myron for the past couple of days, the same way any good hunter pursues an animal. Myron has not been difficult to track. He comes from a prominent and well-known family that owns a chain of prosperous restaurants in each of the province's major cities. The family contributes to a charity that allows the less fortunate to send their kids to music lessons, take part in sporting activities or buy gifts at Christmas time.

Admirable generosity, but local folklore has it that the family accumulated its wealth after winning a high-stakes bet in a basement poker game, right here at Scoundrels. Whether or not it is true, there are still whispers that if you borrow money from the family and it can't be repaid, there will be big trouble. Rumour has it that on more than one occasion, a borrower has had to pay with a property deed.

The Salt family reeks of white privilege: a general advantage that makes it easier for them to cheat anyone out of what is rightfully theirs and get away with it. They just take what they want. Myron was represented by a skilled and expensive lawyer up against an overworked public defender. At the trial, grainy footage showed images of someone who could have been Mavis getting into a grey pickup at a gas station near the outskirts of town. The footage indicated some type of specialty bodywork on the back bumper of the truck—a painting of a yellow honeybee flipping the bird. In the end, the footage was inadmissible because neither the person nor the bodywork was clear enough for a positive ID. This lack of forensic evidence and no eyewitnesses ensured Myron's acquittal. After he was charged, the bee was removed and the truck repainted a dark shade of grey. The Crown requested records of bodywork from the family's own autobody repair shop, but none came up. Family sticks together.

Myron is his parents' third child but unlike the elder siblings who went on to take business training, Myron has been adrift. He skipped classes during his first, second and third years of high school, and eventually dropped out, which his parents passed off as growing pains. When he started snorting cocaine at the age of fifteen, they blamed his social circle and sent him off to rehab, never sitting down with him for a frank discussion or administering any discipline. He's one of those people who has always been afforded the benefit of the doubt.

Wren has stalked Myron enough to piece together a pretty good picture of his life. He works a part-time job in a local convenience store where he makes minimum wage, but not to worry, he's learned to get what he wants. No longer snorting cocaine, he now sells it—a lucrative business that allows him to live alone in a historic, reno-vated war-time home near Scoundrels, where he makes his deals. Each time there's a nod from a stranger amongst the smoke and darkness of this forsaken place, Myron goes to the bathroom, fol-lowed closely by the buyer. Everyone knows that neither are head-ing to the can because they need to pee. Other patrons don't get involved. They've been scared, been hurt, been damaged and are just too blind-drunk to care.

Myron hasn't used ever since he smashed a brand-new car his parents bought him as soon as he got his licence. High as hell at the time, he wrapped it around a telephone pole on the highway. But before the police arrived, he called his parents at four in the morning to come pick him up, which they immediately did. The next day they filed an insurance claim that the car had been stolen. Because of the family's prominence, there were no questions and no consequences. Myron's parents replaced the vehicle within days with a fully loaded SUV. He promised them that he'd stop snorting, and so far he has.

Wren knows all of this because people repeat things they have been told, even if the story was told with the promise of secrecy. Myron likes to brag about things he's done and gotten away with, too, about how he's above the law. Wren discovers where Myron lives from a casual conversation with a new clerk at the convenience store. She also finds out that Myron's new drug of choice is vodka. "He turns up at work so often hungover. Or, I swear, he's still drunk. But hey, the customers seem to like him," gossips the clerk. *Of course they like him*, Wren thinks. *He provides them with blow.*

Wren sits in her car, waiting for him. She is armed with the information the convenience store clerk provided. It's almost showtime.

# ANOMIE

It's nine-thirty in the evening by the time Wren finishes her takeout food and wipes her mouth with a napkin. For the past half hour, she's been staked out in the parking lot, regularly checking her rear-view mirror and see what activity is happening on the street, who is coming and going.

A bag lady wearing black rubber boots wheels a rusted, old shopping cart across the Scoundrel's parking lot toward the dumpster. She's just tall enough to look inside, but she doesn't seem to find anything of interest so she moves on. Wren watches two young boys carrying hockey skates tied together and slung across their shoulders. They walk quickly on the icy sidewalk followed by a medium-sized brown mutt that isn't on a leash. A few cars drive by, most of them older models. The last one Wren saw was missing a back bumper and was obviously in need of a new muffler.

Wren notices a dark figure walking up Pasqua Street. At first, she can't make out his face because every second streetlight in this area has a bulb that is either burned out or smashed. As the person comes closer, Wren can see it's a man. He is wearing a toque, a three-quarter length parka and is tall. He walks with purpose, like he has somewhere important he needs to be.

Wren naturally wonders if this might be Myron. She's been watching him enough lately to know that he has some odd mannerisms. He incessantly picks his nose, for example. Wren thinks about how Myron handles food when he's working at the convenience store. Even though it isn't a restaurant, there are items like hot dogs or beef jerky in a jar, food items that need to be handled by a clerk. As if on cue, Wren sees the walking figure raise his right hand to his nose, dig around, and then flick whatever he's found toward the street. As he comes nearer to the parking lot, she can also begin to see the outline of his face. It's Myron.

Wren is heavily disguised wearing a long, pink and blonde wig and exaggerated makeup like an Egyptian princess. She imagines that Myron's warped sense of entitlement means he thinks can do whatever he wants, including be violent with women—especially brown women like her, many of whom live in the area. He's already proven he can get away with anything.

Wren leaves the safety of her vehicle and follows Myron into the bar. The heavy, wooden door weighs a ton and she has trouble opening it. Once inside, she glances around the dark room for Myron. She catches a glimpse of him and walks over to him. He is already drinking a beer. "Mind if I sit here?" she asks.

"Please do, baby girl," Myron responds, looking her over. "You look just like cotton candy."

Wren takes a seat at an empty table near the bar. Myron moves from his stool to join her. "Can I join you?" he asks.

"Sure," she manages to say through her disgust.

"I'm kind of alone right now," he says. "So thanks."

"I'm just here to meet a friend," she lies. "We were supposed to meet an hour ago, so I've been waiting in the parking lot. She hasn't showed yet, so I thought I'd pop in to see if she came in without me knowing."

"Well, sugar," Myron says, making an attempt at being charming, "I'll be your friend, if you like." He sloshes down the drink he's holding and some of the liquid splashes out on the table.

"Let me get the next round," Wren offers.

"Works for me," he says. "I'll have a vodka."

She walks to the bar in her frilly, silver chiffon shirt and orders. "Double vodka," she says to the woman behind the bar, "and a cranberry juice with soda." Wren slyly examines the area around the bar to see if there are any visible security cameras in place. It makes sense that there should be, but the only camera she sees is facing the cash register, which she stays away from. The young bartender hands Wren the drinks without making eye contact, then continues wiping down the surface of the counter. It seems as though this barkeep has learned the benefits of paying minimal attention.

"Actually, better make that two doubles. My friend seems thirsty tonight."

The barkeep hands over a second drink. "Honey, you need to find yourself a better group of friends."

As the night wears on, Wren continues to purchase drinks for Myron, adding up to about a half-dozen trips to the bar for double shots. Wren always pays in cash, leaving a big tip for the bartender each time. By the time Myron is almost finished his last drink, Wren makes a suggestion: "I think my friend is a no-show tonight, so I might as well just head home. It's been nice sitting with you, but I think it's time to go."

As she reaches for her purse, Myron offers to walk her out to her car.

"I need to have a smoke anyway," he slurs. "May as well walk you out and then maybe head home myself."

It's been over two hours. The clock says it is 11:32 as Myron follows Wren out the front door. She told him she was drinking vodka as well, so Myron believes she's as wasted as he is right now. She didn't give him any personal details all night long. She didn't have to. The entire conversation revolved around how much money he makes, how he plans to make more, and that he just bought a new vehicle.

"I only live a couple of blocks away," he mumbles almost incoherently.

Wren notices a wet spot on Myron's pants. *Holy shit*, she thinks, *he's pissed himself.*

"I say you come home with me and we choke the chicken together," he suggests, unable to stand without swaying in place.

Wren laughs but feels like scratching his eyes out. "Sounds good," she says. "But instead of going to your place, I think you should come home with me. I'll cook you breakfast in the morning."

"Well now that there is a plan," he agrees, trying to light a cigarette. He's having problems with the childproof lighter. *Not surprising,* Wren thinks to herself as she grabs the lighter from his hands and flicks it to spark.

She has to hold him up as they walk to her car. Wren opens her car door and helps her drunken victim into the passenger seat, thinking only about purging the world of filth. Like getting rid of aphids or slugs, she muses, looking at his glassy eyes and swollen mouth. And wet pants. Wren suddenly stops assisting him into the vehicle. "I have a dog who sheds a lot and I don't want you to get covered with fur," she lies. "So just a second. I'll grab a blanket and put it over your seat as a cover." She carries a blanket in her car because Lord insists, just in case she finds herself stuck sometime.

"Oh, sure, thanks," Myron replies.

Wren isn't sure he even knows what she just said. Once he's in and buckled up, she offers him some Gatorade.

"You'll want to drink this. It'll help you not have a hangover in the morning."

"Oh, okay," Myron says, taking the drink. He takes down the liquid, laced with several crushed-up blue pills, in one big gulp. He is passed out by the time Wren pulls into her long, dark driveway.

# AMID FRENZY AND CONDEMNATION

Wren uses all her strength to pull Myron's body from the passenger seat of her car. He lands with a thud, hitting his head on the cobblestone walkway to the house. Wren curses at herself for being so careless. She remembers the time when Mooshum helped young Wren and her sister plant lollipops in the cracks. Wren shudders at the thought that Myron's body has touched these stones.

From somewhere deep inside her, a most violent creature that Wren doesn't even recognize emerges and it is enraged. She is disgusted at having to handle this worthless piece of skin and feels compelled to kick Myron in the head. She puts her boot to his temple, not once or twice, but five times. Myron's nose begins to bleed, and she kicks him again, even harder along his torso. Wren hears his ribs breaking under the coat he's wearing. She is sickened by the sight of his stinking, bleeding body splayed out on the ground, drunk and unconscious.

Whatever force has overtaken her is still strong and in control. There are still a couple of vials of insulin hidden in her art supplies, but this time she elects not to make the trip to get them. Instead, she stops in the bathroom and grabs a full bottle of household bleach and a new syringe. She cannot lose the image of that young girl terrorized and slashed before being shoved under a bale of hay. Wren decides she will inflict the same level of anguish upon Myron. She decides he needs to feel pain and suffering for what he's done. He deserves to shudder in agony as the bleach burns his veins and breaks arteries.

"No forensic evidence," she mutters.

Wren's hand is steady as she fills the syringe with the potent liquid. She heads back outdoors where she hears only the sound of wind.

Wren knows that Myron's body is likely to convulse as she slowly injects the bleach into his neck, the same part of Mavis's body that he slashed. In her frenzied anger, Wren decides she'd also like this fucker to know what not being able to breathe feels like.

She returns to her car and reaches into her glove box where she keeps a can of pepper spray. Wren sometimes carries it with her when walking by herself, something Lord insists on even though coyotes have never come close enough to her to cause concern. Wren sprays the noxious mist directly up Myron's nostrils and is startled when he opens his bloodshot eyes. He claws at his nose, gasping and scratching.

"You will harm no more," Wren says aloud before injecting him again with a second dose of bleach. He flops on the ground for about a minute and then his body goes limp.

Once more, she remembers the butcher knife that she saw in her vision. The one he used to slash the girl's throat. Wren goes back into the farmhouse to retrieve her sharpest knife, the one she's used so many times to prepare a family meal. By the time she returns, Myron is dead. He has no pulse and there is a white froth coming from his nose and mouth. Wren pulls off the Nike running shoes from his feet.

"Stupid ass, don't even dress properly for the cold," she hisses.

Another trophy. She cuts off the blue jeans he's wearing, not caring if the cutting means slashing his foul legs.

Wren had fed kindling and several small logs of wood into the outdoor kiln before she went stalking. Now, standing here under the bright light of a full moon, she says a prayer—not for Myron, but to Grandmother Moon. She asks her to care for the soul of the young girl who was murdered, just as Wren will take care of Myron, ridding him from the Earth so he can never cause harm again.

Wren throws more logs into the kiln before shoving Myron's body in. In this moment, something snaps within her again. She looks at the snow. Red with hate. She urgently wants to drain more of his blood. Wren finds herself going for the axe leaning against the side of the farmhouse. She will dismember this foul body and feed it to the fire. Allowing rigor mortis to set in this time seems too kind for what he's done, for how he has violated and sinned.

As she hacks, hearing bones split, she wonders if burning the remains of this poisoned soul might have the same effect as burning poison ivy. Plant experts advise never to do it. The toxic spores of the weed are just as dangerous if they become airborne, as they would be with direct contact on the skin. *And*, Wren wonders, *can a poison be planted within a person's mind?* Again, she prays to Grandmother Moon that Myron's kind of poison will be eliminated here and now, once and for all, airborne or otherwise.

Wren angrily tosses the piss-stained blanket from her passenger seat into the kiln. Next, she hurls leg parts, arms and a head into the hearth. Looking into the darkness of night, she notices the coyote. He is witness again to things unspoken. He keeps his distance, but she can see his luminous eyes reflect the moonlight. And those eyes are hungry.

"I will create some more pottery," she says. "More gargoyles, with a prayer to ward off the evil that is you. Invasive and poisonous species, you shall cause harm no more."

The fouled snow will have to be disposed. Wren's first thought is to go to her studio and grab a couple of gunny sacks and a shovel. The forensic evidence can be dumped in the gully. It will be further covered by flurries, which are sure to fall as the winter progresses. It will disappear, seeping into the ground come springtime.

But her tirade has left Wren exhausted. She figures she can wait until morning to take care of this cumbersome detail. She lights the flame and waits for a spark before picking up her Ginsu and slowly heading back toward the farmhouse. As she walks, she can hear the wood spit and crackle.

# ASSURANCE

By the next morning, not even small whiffs of smoke drift anymore from the small chimney of the outdoor kiln. She'll have to go out and stoke the fire repeatedly over the next forty-eight hours, but in these silent moments of early morning, that detail can wait a little bit longer.

Over the past several hours, Wren has been laying on the couch, bundled up in the colourful, woollen afghan that covered her and her husband the night they danced and slept in front of the fireplace in the living room. She has been drifting in and out of restless sleep. Along with Myron, she also burned the pink wig, skirt and sequined, butterfly-adorned top that she wore to Scoundrels. An exhausting ordeal. Wren's been waiting for the fire to take him, wanting to be sure it all happens over the next couple of days before her husband returns.

During the moments when her conscious mind travelled elsewhere, Wren saw the "jumpers" coming, a term she always used to describe the mythical creatures her kohkum would sometimes talk about. They are nocturnal, about the size of a fox, and they stand upright with strong legs that resemble those of a grasshopper. Their bulging eyes are keener than a cat's, and maybe like a cat, they can look directly into a person's soul.

According to Kohkum's story, the jumpers live underground and prefer a den that's close to water. Wild cucumbers are their main source of food. They will also eat flesh, though, with their razor-sharp fangs that come out when they sense impure thoughts. Jumpers are like janitors, scrubbing the land of waste and ruin. Their bodies are sleek and opaque like the underbelly of a white fish. The jumpers are covered with scales and have small-but-deadly arms that look like those of a giant praying mantis.

Wren recalls a story about what jumpers will do if they sense danger is present. Kohkum talked about an evil drifter, a Young Dog or Young Dog offspring. His mind was filthy and his hands were dirty. He was hiding in the dark waiting for parents to go to sleep before dousing a ragged cloth with chloroform. His heart raced as he sat waiting, waiting, waiting for his chance to turn back the canvas flap of a tent where two young girls slept in the backyard.

He'd be quiet and those girls would end up raped and dead, except that the jumpers caught wind of him. They knew what was in his heart and in his troubled mind. They knew and they acted. As the drifter slowly approached the tent, the jumpers followed, watching him from their perch atop nearby trees. Three jumpers came that night, silently as they always do, and surrounded that evil man.

He became paralyzed with fear when he saw them. They slashed his wretched body, tearing away limbs, dismembering his guts, all without making a sound, without leaving a trace, and with the precision of skilled hunters. They took the body parts and planted them near their den—food for the roots of the bulrushes as well as for the fish and frogs.

But those jumpers are not to be feared. They don't harm unless there is need to do so. Wren's mental wandering takes her back to her own childhood, her own memory. She and Raven had a couple of friends stay for a sleepover. They'd had a big bonfire for a marshmallow and wiener roast. There was no curfew, but Kohkum told them to go to sleep in the big canvas tent when they got tired. They stayed up late, long enough to see the total darkness of the night sky, but not before finishing a whole bag of marshmallows, some of the soft, sweet bits falling to the ground in their gleeful haste.

Sometime before daybreak, Wren had to go to the bathroom, so she quietly crept out from under her sleeping bag, careful not to disturb her sleeping mates. The bonfire had simmered to embers, although still offered a soft light. When Wren opened the tent flap, she saw a jumper sitting near the firepit, eating the marshmallows bits that were left on the ground.

At first she was frightened upon seeing this mysterious creature with shiny white skin, but it looked over at her with big, round eyes and without speaking, told her not to be afraid. He conveyed that he was staying the night to keep watch over the girls, to be sure they were all safe. Then in a flash, the thing vanished into the treetops, leaving the young Wren with a sense of safety, a knowing that she is never alone. She's sure now that she's felt that jumper's energy around her many times since.

In her visions tonight as she lays on the couch, she can see jumpers circling the kiln and dancing, just as she did the last time she turned someone to bone-black ash. The image startles Wren awake, and she goes to the kitchen to splash some cold water on her face. Wren decides to make herself a tea and wait for first light before finishing the job and cleaning up. There was so much blood when she chopped Myron to pieces; forensic evidence all over the place was something she never intended.

# REDEMPTION

As she stares at her latest work of pottery, Wren wonders if she will eventually find her way out of this quagmire in her life. The pottery stares back at her: the fool with a gargoyle's face. The sculpture shows similar facial features to that of a Neanderthal man, with a sloped chin and forehead. She's carved Medusa-like snakes in place of hair because the myth surrounding this guardian warns that anyone who might gaze into her eyes will turn to stone.

Myron Salt has turned to stone. Medusa's hair will keep him in check, even in death, ensuring that he no longer brings harm to women. Once this piece is fired in the kiln, Wren will use Myron's bone ash to glaze the piece with a black finish. She runs a cutting wire under the wet clay to loosen it from the round piece of wood it's sitting on. As she carefully lifts it, Wren notices the piece is heavier than she expected, much the same as the night she dragged Myron's body from the passenger seat of her car.

Wren's movements are precise and meticulous as she gently lowers the gargoyle into her studio kiln. She'll fire it to 1800 degrees. Because of its height, twenty inches, it will have to bake for eight hours. It'll take another day after that to let the kiln cool down enough for her to remove the piece. Not a fast process. Once she glazes it, she'll need to fire it for another ten hours, then let it cool for two days. She'll sand the bottom after that.

After setting the kiln's temperature, Wren shakes her head. She had left Myron's blood in the snow. She didn't clean up the blood directly in front of the outdoor kiln either, because she had been too tired, too overwhelmed. The area must have resembled the floor of a slaughterhouse.

Early the following morning though, when she went out to clean the mess at daybreak, everything looked serene. There were no splatter marks or pools of blood, just the pristine white of freshly fallen snow. It was as if by magic. As though someone had been enlisted to come in and take care of the mess. Jumpers?

Wren's not completely sure. She wonders if she cleaned up herself and simply forgot she'd done it. She's been tired and disoriented lately, so it's possible. Her mind has been at war with Kohkum's teachings, notions of good grace, kindness and forgiveness. She now smudges each day, asking for redemption, clarity and some sort of sign that what she's been doing is more of a service than a sin.

At this moment, an image of her sister's pretty face comes to mind. Wren decides to turn on the radio and listen to some morning talk. The breaking story all over the news is that of a young man missing in Regina's North Central. His family is offering a generous reward for any information that might lead to his whereabouts. Wren scoffs. "There is no evidence and no eyewitnesses," she mutters.

While her kiln hums away hardening the clay, there is other work to do. Wren has received a custom order from the province's Office of Protocol. Since her exhibit, word has spread about the uniqueness of her designs. The Office likes to promote its own Saskatchewan artists, so an order was placed for one of her clay cooking pots as a gift for a visiting dignitary. The design Wren has chosen shows a lake scene surrounded by the Qu'Appelle Valley's rolling hills. It has been glazed in a bone black finish.

She needs to get it wrapped and boxed up as she promised them delivery yesterday. As she reaches for the clay pot, it makes her think about cooking, and that she will have to get to that chore this morning as well. Wren's got all the ingredients in her fridge to make another quiche. She'll caramelize some onions, ham and cheese, and add a sprinkling of saffron. It's become Lord's favourite dish and he is coming home today: Valentine's Day.

Wren is proud of her husband's accomplishments. His architectural design for renovating the heritage building in Winnipeg was accepted. Everything is in place and the job is underway. Wren wants to celebrate, which is why she went to the grocery store yesterday to pick up every type of fruit they had in stock. Lord loves fruit salad, especially with strawberries. She'll serve it with fresh whipped cream. It thrills Wren to plan out the time she spends with her husband.

After packaging the Office of Protocol's clay pot, Wren feels nauseated. The feeling strikes her quickly. There is no time to run back into the farmhouse and to the upstairs bathroom, so Wren yanks open the front door of her studio and hangs her head outside. Pain. Vomit. She wipes the remnants of spittle from her mouth using the apron she's wearing. Wren hasn't felt any onset of illness even though it is flu season. She hasn't had sniffles, congestion or fever. She realizes then that just thinking about the smell of preparing a quiche—cutting onions and whisking eggs—triggered her nausea. She pukes one more time.

# NO MORE SECRETS

It is early afternoon when Wren sees a black Ford Bronco slow down on the highway, readying to turn down the long driveway toward the farmhouse. The vehicle is unfamiliar to her and for a second it causes Wren to worry. She wonders if someone, somewhere has figured out what she's been up to. She's been watching out the window for her husband's car, glancing toward the roadway every few minutes. Wren doesn't want any strangers dropping in unexpectedly on her special day. She's already prepared a meal, showered and freshened up. She even dabbed some perfume on each side of her neck.

She watches as the unknown vehicle pulls closer toward the farmhouse, then come to a stop, parking just beside the cobblestone walkway. Any feelings of dread are immediately erased as Lord steps out of the Bronco holding a bouquet of flowers, the same type of mixed bouquet he gave Wren on their first date. Wren quickly opens the door and runs in for a bear hug. It's cold out and she isn't wearing a winter jacket but that doesn't bother her.

"Oh my god! I'm so glad you're home," she says, burying her face in his chest. "What's with the new vehicle?"

"Oh, my love. Always with the questions." Lord kisses his wife on the forehead. "Let's go inside. You're going to freeze out here with no coat." Once indoors, he hands over the flowers. "I know they say that roses are the perfect gift for Valentine's, but I think this bouquet is better. Always reminds me of our first date."

Wren smiles from ear to ear and begins looking through the cupboards for a suitable vase.

"One of the sponsors for the renovation is from a bigger car dealership in the 'Peg, so I traded in my car and drove home in style.

I think I got the family discount," Lord says and laughs. "And you? What have you been up to while I've been away?"

Wren tells him she's been spending a lot of time in her studio working on new pieces.

"With your encouragement, I made another one of those gargoyles and a few other new pieces. I'm happy with the outcome. Now sit, you must be hungry," she says, pulling out a chair.

She serves him a piece of quiche, but before taking a bite, Lord has another surprise for Wren. He reaches into the chest pocket of his dress shirt and produces the most exquisite pair of amethyst earrings. Studs that sparkle.

"I know how much you loved that necklace I brought home last time I went away. Thought these would pair with it nicely."

"I love them," Wren squeals, holding the purple, polished stones in her palm. "I love *you*."

As always, Lord's kindness reminds Wren that there's so much goodness in the world. Her husband is generous, loving and kind. She begins to sob. Lord wraps her in his arms.

"What's wrong, my love?"

"I can't keep secrets from you anymore," she responds.

Lord's muscles become rigid, as does his expression. This is the type of statement that usually means bad news. He always carries a photo of Wren when he travels and without fail, work colleagues comment that he should be spending more time at home. Lord wipes away a tear that is slowly rolling down Wren's cheek and waits for her to explain.

"It's nothing bad," she begins. "It's just that last time this happened I didn't tell you and that's something I regret. I should have told you."

"What are you talking about, Wren?"

"I've been feeling sick lately. And my period is late."

"Oh, that's wonderful news!" Lord brightens up and begins to plan. "I can renovate the baby's room. You pick the colours, of course." He smiles at his wife and gently holds her hand as though she's something so delicate he worries she'll break.

Wren's expression changes from worried to uplifted, but she warns, "Remember last time, though? I didn't tell you because it sometimes happens that babies go away. It's all been so much, my love, but now I think God is smiling on us."

"This is the most wonderful news in the world. Do you know for sure?" he asks.

"Well, no, I don't. I just suspect I am because I threw up this morning for no reason. It's usually an indicator. I guess I'll make a doctor's appointment as soon as possible."

"Who wants to wait that long?" Lord exclaims. "I say we get back into my new Bronco right now, drive to the drug store and pick up one of those tests."

Wren tries to explain that home pregnancy tests are not always accurate, but that doesn't seem to concern Lord. He grabs a piece of quiche from the kitchen island to snack on as the two make their way to the vehicle.

# PONDERANCE AND SUPERSTITION

With out-of-town projects well underway, Lord elects to stay close to home. The pregnancy test showed a positive result and that very afternoon, Lord insists that he and Wren head to the city for some baby furniture. To calm his wife's concerns about faulty results, he also suggests that the couple go to a walk-in medical clinic to have a blood test done. The smiling family physician made it official that afternoon: the couple is expecting a baby.

Since that moment, Lord has been treating Wren like a precious treasure. He has forbidden her from moving heavy objects and hires a house cleaner to come in once a week, over Wren's objections. He goes with her when she's shopping for food because he doesn't want her to carry bags that might be too heavy. He buys jugs of milk every couple of days, which makes him chuckle because Wren has never been a big milk drinker until now. He's happy to know his wife has a craving for calcium which is good for a baby's growth. He's even learned to cook.

The first trimester comes and goes without upset, and Lord accompanies Wren to each checkup with the doctor. The baby is growing well and Wren is now showing. It takes all his effort for Lord not to caress his wife's belly each time he sees her. Choosing paint colours for the baby's room has not been an easy task but there is no question that that old wallpaper in the spare room must go. Dated and yellowed by the passage of time, neither Wren nor Lord want their beautiful baby to wake up to it each day. After some discussion, the baby's room will be painted the colour of the sky, the colour of infinity and hope, a shade called "Blue Lagoon."

Before any colour is added, however, the hardwood floor is in need of some care. The room is pretty empty, with only an old dresser and a few boxes filled with old books needing to be moved. As Lord opens one of the boxes, he is filled with contentment upon seeing a copy of Dr. Seuss's *Green Eggs and Ham*. He figures it's something Wren often read as a child and he removes the book from its place, hidden in a box. It will be a part of their baby's life, too. Lord smiles as he imagines sitting on the bed and reading a book to his child. He makes a point of taking the copy and walking it down the hallway where he sets it on his bedside table. He knows it's a memory that will make his wife happy.

Back in the baby's room, Lord opens a dresser drawer. He finds the death photo of his mother hidden underneath some scarves. Hidden from sight by his wife.

# BANISH THEE

Lord has come down to the kitchen where Wren is making some tea. He's carrying the photo of his dead mother lying in her coffin. "Why did I find this hidden in the spare room?"

"Oh that." Wren feels a twinge of guilt. "How can I explain?" she starts.

She admits her fear, that the Magras curse might be something real, kept alive, if only in the imagination. Wren tells Lord that something about that photo seems wrong to her. Haunting, as if his mother still doesn't want anyone to enter their home. She talks about how the couple has not had any visitors except for Raven, but that Raven went away. And that first baby, too.

Wren tells Lord about the dreams she's been having about a scarecrow, and that it is somehow influencing her not allow anyone across the threshold of the farmhouse. She tells him she worries for the new baby, and that somehow that photo of his mother might be trying to undo what happiness they have found.

"It is just a photo, Wren." Lord does his best to console his wife, though he is upset that she hid the picture in a drawer.

"A photo, yes," Wren replies, "but what if, somehow, your mom attached a part of herself to the photo? What if the curse is not just something that was talked about, but something real? I can't risk losing another baby, Lord."

Wren continues, trying to explain the intensity of her fears so Lord will understand. She describes a memory from her childhood, standing alone on the prairie near an abandoned farmhouse, its wood rotting with age and weather. "There are voices that can be heard from its cistern. And a smell, like sour flesh. There was always something about that place that said *Stay away*. Raven and I went there on our bikes sometimes when we were girls, even though we were warned not to."

The prairie area is near the lake, within walking distance of the point. Wren talks about an old hermit who used to live there who died in his sleep and no one found him for months. He had not picked up his mail all those weeks, which is why the post office alerted police to go and check. By the time the RCMP showed up, he'd already been wrapped in cobwebs and was stiff and rotted. The whole house was filled with spiders. In life, that man hated and cursed anyone who crossed his path. The story says he ended up like that because he was jilted by his young bride, who left him with no explanation. His heart went to darkness and he called on a curse. He believed in it and gave it life.

After he died, the property stood empty. Nothing grew except for weeds. Wren remembers feeling like there was electricity in the air whenever she went near the home. Raven and Wren dared each other but never went in, prevented by a foreboding feeling of being watched. "So, I do believe in curses. People make fun of it and call it nothing but superstition," Wren tells Lord, "but I really think that if you give a bad thought too much energy, it becomes something real. And by its very nature, a curse does nothing but cause harm. I can't take that chance now."

As she holds her belly, Lord softens towards her. He realizes that there have not been many guests invited into this farmhouse. Raven did disappear and yes, the first baby went away. He wonders if his wife is correct, that lending thought to an ominous suggestion gives it power, transforms it from an idea into a true thing. He decides in that moment that if something was done, it can be undone.

"I will get rid of the photo," he says. "Out of the house. I will burn it and send my mother's intention away with it. Then she can rest in peace. But I will need your help."

# SPRING MELT

Thoughts of revenge and vengeance no longer cloud her mind. Her pregnancy is now in its second trimester and the couple couldn't be more excited. Lord has painted the baby's room and put up some stained glass in the window. The colourful glass faces west, so the baby will be covered with light as the sun goes down, marking each day in colour. Wren's appetite has returned and Lord is doing much of the cooking, although he still stops in frequently at a deli in the city to get to-go meals. Wren is aglow, happy and looking forward to the future. She suggests taking a road trip before the baby arrives.

"I've been thinking about our earlier discussions about taking a trip abroad," Wren tells Lord, "but it occurs to me that we don't need to leave home to find something more magical than what we already have right here in Saskatchewan." Lord doesn't quite follow, so Wren explains further. "We can go to Amsterdam or Strasbourg and never have to leave the ground. Never have to travel elsewhere," she continues. "There are all sorts of towns named after international cities right here in this province." She laughs. "Let's see how the local folk in those places live. Let's find out their local customs and what they do. We can even visit Norway and the Hague, just outside of Saskatoon." Wren snickers, adding, "Besides, I don't want to fly away somewhere if there might be problems with the baby is all I'm saying."

"A road trip?" Lord inquires.

"A road trip, yes," Wren replies. "How many people know you can visit Kandahar without ever having to board a flight? We have that town right here in the province." At this she pats her tummy and says, "I bet they have great snacks in Penzance. Let's give this baby an appreciation of history about the place we call home. A history that is both yours and mine.

She goes on to talk about the prairie landscape and how it changes from farmland to lakes and bush, to Precambrian Shield and the boreal forest. Wren talks about how food traditions change along the way, too, from Russian shishliki lamb, to Icelandic jólasveinar sausage. She talks about flapper pie, raisin pie and all the different ways bread is made, adding the suggestion that they stop in at various Indigenous-owned gas stations to pick up fried bannock.

Lord nods his head in agreement, not fully knowing what he is agreeing to.

"We'll be together. Just you and me," she continues. "Hours and hours on the road. We can listen to seventies music all the while stopping whenever we want because we are not in a hurry. We can take photos, talk, eat home-baked goods."

His wife has had a generous appetite lately, which makes him feel assured and joyous.

Wren adds, "It doesn't matter if we spend each night in a cheap roadside motel. We'll get to know the land and the people we live with, those we call our neighbours. This province where we live is multi-layered, like my pottery pieces. We are bringing a new life into this world, and I want her to know her world. I want her to be interested in stories about local museums and the people who live down the road, even if that road is hours away. It's how we understand why we do what we do; it's how we make sense."

Wren holds her husband's hand, a gesture of hope that he'll get more excited about it. "And how about checking out the architecture that has been imported from elsewhere in the world and is now part of this prairie landscape?"

Finally a comment that piques Lord's interest. He has only ever seen photos of stone buildings or sod houses across the plains. He's looked at pictures of train trestle bridges and the wonder of that engineering, but has never seen them up close. He's driven by grain elevators which stand as sentinels of the past in many towns. Those structures were crucial in building this province, keeping families fed at one point in time. He admits to himself he would like to see those old ones up close before they're taken by the wind and the weather. But mostly, he's persuaded to do this because of his wife. She beams with excitement at the plan.

Wren pats her tummy again. "We'll have fun, just, well, just *being*. I love you more than words can say. Please say yes."

Lord agrees to the road trip. He knows it will include drinking a great deal of gas station coffees, which will likely come with their own stories. He knows that a road trip like this means driving for hours and hours with nothing but wild grasslands, buttes filled with native bush and flora, and harvested crops. He and Wren will be exploring together, celebrating things that are ordinary but somehow extraordinary. Things like finding delightful greasy-spoon diners and wandering around main streets. They both know that a baby is always seen as a blessing, and this trip will be her introductory welcome to the world.

Wren heads outside, and as she sits beside the trickling creek, she listens to the sound of melting ice breaking and says a prayer. It's a conflicting notion, but she can't help but wonder if she is somehow being rewarded for taking care of business and ridding the world of those who caused harm. In this joyful time, she makes a solemn promise to no longer take part in the chaos of this world. To walk along a pathway of love and light. To travel in grace.

"Please let this baby enter this world as a protected soul who doesn't lose her way," Wren whispers to the river.

Wren is hoping the child will be a girl. She always refers to it as *she* even though the couple has elected not to know the sex. Wren's already decided she will name the baby after Raven. She will share with this child a love of the land and repeat the stories told to her so many years ago by her beloved kohkum. She will be gentle and kind and protect this baby from harm.

Wren goes back to the farmhouse and smudges with what is left of the dried sage she picked late last summer, the last afternoon she was able to run with her sister toward the bluff, covered in a meadow of wildflowers. The last time they lay amongst the tall prairie grass and watched the clouds. The last time she remembers that all things were good in this world.

She feels her baby kick. Wren strokes her tummy, feeling blessed that balance in her life has finally returned. But a craving has also returned. She's been eating the cinnamon buns that are baked each morning at the local gas station, sometimes twice a day. Wren stands up and loosens some dried grass from her skirt before deciding to head into town.

"There's a bun in the oven with my name on it." She giggles at her own bad joke and calls into the house, "Want to come with me? I'm going to make a trip to the gas station again."

He declines, saying there are some emails that need attention, but it doesn't break Wren's resolve. She is feeling happy, like good in the world is coming. And besides, she can buy an extra cinnamon bun for him and bring it home.

As she walks down the pathway and towards her car, Wren notices the coyote watching from a distance. He hasn't been around for a while. He's pacing and seems frantic with purpose. Wren gives him a wave, saying, "Hello, old friend. I have nothing for you today, but if you want, I can pick up an extra bun while I am in town. I will leave it in the gully for you when I get back." The coyote follows her more closely, halfway up the pathway, before hearing traffic on the highway and retreating into the bush.

During her short drive into town, Wren thinks about ways in which she has conducted her own ceremony of letting go. Under the full light of Grandmother Moon, she danced around the fire. She burned the newspaper articles that told the stories of Father Hector and Myron Salt to let that poison go. She said a prayer and offered it to the fire. She gave thanks for all the people who've come into her life and helped by offering friendship and guidance, then burned some photos. The first was of her sister. She still gets weepy at the thought that Raven may never be found, and the mystery of her disappearance may never be solved, just like no one will ever find Father Hector, Billy Vespas or Myron Salt.

Wren has been using this time during the baby's growth to try and heal her own heart and always, to remember the bond she had with Raven. They shared a sacred space together—in utero, like the baby is now, and through all those years of growing and learning. Wren also burned that photo of Lord's mother laying in her coffin. She offered food for the old woman's spirit, hoping it nourishes her and carries her to a place where fear exists no more.

The farmhouse seems more at peace as well. There's a familiar energy, like she remembers when she was growing up. Kohkum's love has returned. The morning light is brighter when it shines through her kitchen window and the old wooden stairs no longer creak. And Lord? He seems to have lost his angst about inviting people over. A curse removed forever, Wren hopes. She smiles, remembering last weekend when Lord invited work colleagues to come over for brunch in celebration of their impending arrival. A secondary purpose was to help create a new design he'd imagined for the baby's crib: repurposed barn wood that would be covered with an old quilt from his childhood. She was surprised Lord insisted on preparing brunch that day: fry bread and Spam along with a lush fruit salad that included many plump strawberries.

Wren's happy musings come to an abrupt halt as she pulls into the gas station parking lot. Wren sees a blue pickup truck with silver bull's balls hanging from the back hitch. It isn't owned by a local resident, Wren is sure. No one out here would drive around with a bumper sticker proclaiming, *Rednecks Rule.*

Something in Wren begins to stir again. In her mind, she is transported back to the ditch. Blood is in her hair and scalp. She's on her bike, looking for her sister. In that moment, a stillness sets in. Even the wind stops blowing. No breeze, just calm and clarity. Wren is transported to a dream state, a place bereft of colour, and a feeling that she is floating on air. It's in this place that she catches a glimpse of her sister, who is smiling. Raven gently reaches out to touch Wren's cheek and everything starts to unravel.

The wind blows Wren back to the present, where she finds herself standing in the gas station parking lot, startled by loud squawking. There is a flurry of activity in a nearby tree where a murder of crows has landed. Wren counts seven birds and wonders if their arrival signals action, a cackling suggestion from the souls of those departed. A large, grand raven flies in like a sentinel and takes a spot at the top of the aspen. The raven looks directly at Wren and squawks loudly, as if calling her to arms.

Wren is sure she knows what it means. As she casts a glance toward a pale blue and cloudless sky, she rubs her hands together and looks back at the pickup with those bull balls and the same licence plate number she had committed to memory many months ago. She crosses her fingers and makes the sign of the cross over her head and her heart.

"One more," she says to no one.

# NOTES & ACKNOWLEDGEMENTS

The "Young Dogs" in the text was first referenced in the 1913 publication of *The Company of Adventurers* by Isaac Cowie.

✳ ✳ ✳

Sending special recognition to my three beautiful children: Jackson, Nahanni and Daniel.

Thank you to the following people for help with Cree translation and expertise on pottery techniques, suggestions and encouragement: Neal McLeod, Karlie King, Barbara Goretzky, Janice Lentowicz, Kari Lentowicz, Carol Draper, Lori Zak, Alice Marvin, Neil Marvin, Kathleen Coleclough, Rae Pelletier, Linda Ford, Jeannie Leblond, Andino Suns, Andres Davalos, Kristin Teetaert, Larry Hall, Tracey George-Hesse, Trevor Herriot, Lorna Standing Ready, Linda Lyster, Alex Bodnarchuk, Michelle Lenuik, Terri Boldt (otherwise affectionately known as "Trouble"— lol), Shawna Lemay, Krista Schultz, Karen Wheeler, and of course to my publisher Silas White and my editor Amber McMillan. I also wish to send gratitude to arts organizations that allow for artists to create, such as the Canada Council for the Arts, the Saskatchewan Arts Board, Saskatchewan Cultural Exchange (thanks to John Kennedy and his lovely wife Debra Bell), the Saskatchewan Foundation for the Arts, the Saskatchewan Writers' Guild, Last Mountain Lake Cultural Centre, SaskCulture and Creative Saskatchewan.

# ABOUT THE AUTHOR

**Carol Rose GoldenEagle** (previously Carol Daniels) is a Saskatchewan author of the novel *Bearskin Diary*, chosen as the Aboriginal Literature Title for 2017 and shortlisted for three Saskatchewan Book Awards in 2018. Her French-language translation of the same novel, *Peau D'ours*, won the 2019 Saskatchewan Book Award, Prix du livre français. Her first book of poetry, *Hiraeth*, was shortlisted for a Saskatchewan Book Award in 2019. GoldenEagle is an Aboriginal artist, multi-disciplined in the areas of writing, storytelling, singing, drumming and visual art.